JAN 3 0 2020

P9-DZP-156

NAPA COUNTY LIBRARY
580 COOMBS STREET
NAPA, CA 94559

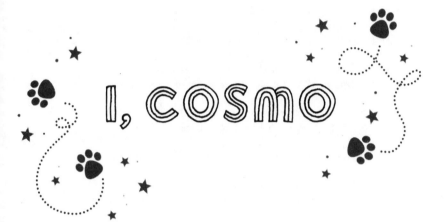

Carlie Sorosiak

WALKER BOOKS

Text copyright © 2019 by Carlie Sorosiak

All rights reserved. No part of this book may be reproduced, transmitted, or stored in an information retrieval system in any form or by any means, graphic, electronic, or mechanical, including photocopying, taping, and recording, without prior written permission from the publisher.

First U.S. edition 2019
First published by Nosy Crow (U.K.) 2019

Library of Congress Catalog Card Number 2019939648
ISBN 978-1-5362-0769-9

19 20 21 22 23 24 LBM 10 9 8 7 6 5 4 3 2 1

Printed in Melrose Park, IL

This book was typeset in New Century Schoolbook.

Walker Books US
a division of
Candlewick Press
99 Dover Street
Somerville, Massachusetts 02144

www.walkerbooksus.com

MIX
From responsible
sources
FSC® C103098

To all the dogs I've ever loved, and very much still do, especially Ralphie, Sally, Dany, Buddy, Faith, Chloe, Mary Jane, and Oscar.

How can we know the dancer
from the dance?

—*William Butler Yeats*

This year I am a turtle. I do not want to be a turtle.

"His tail's between his legs," Max notes, cocking his head. Worry spreads across his wonderful face. "You think the hat's too tight?"

We are on the porch, and the strange pumpkin is smiling at us—the one Max carved last week, scooping out its guts. I ate the seeds even though he told me "No, Cosmo, no." I find it difficult to stop myself when something smells so interesting and so new.

Max's father, whose name is Dad, readjusts the turtle vest on my back. "Nah, he's fine. He loves it! Look at him!"

This is one of those times—those infinite

times—when I wish my tongue did not loll in my mouth. Because I would say, in perfect human language, that turtles are inferior creatures who cannot manage to cross roads, and I have crossed many roads, off-leash, by myself. This costume is an embarrassment.

At a loss, I roll gently onto my back, kicking my legs in the air. An ache creaks down my spine; I am not young like I used to be. But hopefully Max will understand the subtle meaning in my gesture.

"Dad, I *really* think he doesn't like it."

Yes, Max! Yes!

Scratching the fur on his chin, Dad says to me, "Okay, okay, no hat, but you've gotta keep the shell."

And just like that, a small victory.

Emmaline bursts onto the porch then. She is all energy. She glows. *"Cosmooooo."* Her little hands ruffle my ears, and it reminds me why I am a turtle in the first place—because Emmaline picked it out. Because it made her happy. I've long accepted that this is one of my roles.

Max grabs Emmaline's hand and spins her around, like they're dancing. Her purple superhero cape twirls with the movement. Last week, I helped Mom make the costume: guarding the fabric, keeping watch by her feet, and every once and a while,

she held up her progress and asked me, "Whaddya think, Cosmo?"

A wonder, I told her with my eyes. *It is a wonder.*

"Shouldn't we wait for Mom?" Max asks. He is dressed in dark colors, patches on his shirt, and I suppose he is a cow or a giraffe, although I do not like thinking of him as either. Giraffes are remarkably stupid creatures, and Max is very, very smart. He can speak three languages, build model rockets, and fold his tongue into a four-leaf clover. He can even unscrew the lids off peanut butter jars. I'd like to see a giraffe do *that.*

Dad replies, "She's late. Don't want to miss all the good candy."

Max says, "I just think—"

But Dad cuts him off with "Ready, Freddy," which he is fond of saying, despite the fact that Max is called Max. After a pause, the four of us set off into the bluish night. Our house is a one-story brick structure with plenty of grass and a swing set that only Emmaline uses now. Paper lanterns line the driveway, lighting up the cul-de-sac.

The fur on the back of my neck begins to rise.

Halloween is the worst night of the year. If you disagree, please take a moment to consider my logic:

3

1. Most Halloween candy is chocolate. My fourth Halloween, I consumed six miniature Hershey's bars and was immediately rushed to the emergency vet, where I spent four hours with an incredible tummy ache.

2. Young humans jump out from behind bushes and yell *"Boo!"* This is confusing. One of my best friends, a German shorthaired pointer, is named Boo.

3. Clowns.

4. Golden retrievers, like myself, are too dignified for costumes. I am not entirely opposed to raincoats if the occasion arises, but there is a line. For example, Mom bought me a cat costume once, and I have yet to wholly recover from the trauma.

5. The sheepdog is let loose.

Allow me to elaborate on this fifth point. I have never had an appetite for confrontation—not even when I was a puppy. But I make an exception for the sheepdog.

Five Halloweens ago, on a night just like this, Max and I approached a white-shingled house at the end of the street. A big, blocky van idled by the mailbox, and a roast-chicken smell wafted from two open windows. I knew immediately that we had new neighbors—the old neighbors were strictly beef-eaters. An eerie quietness settled over the street, a dark cloud moving to block the moon. So quick that I did not even see it coming, the sheepdog emerged from behind a massive oak tree in their front yard. It was wearing an ominous pink tutu and fairy wings, its gray-and-white fur standing on end.

My immediate reaction was empathy—hadn't we both succumbed to the same costumed fate? I began to trot over in my bunny outfit, intent on bowing in commiseration, and then welcoming it to the neighborhood with a friendly sniff of its butt. What happened next was not friendly. I have never seen anything like it in my thirteen years.

The sheepdog bared its teeth, a menacing snarl directed straight at me . . . And I swear its eyes glowed red.

I was horrified.

There are few things that truly frighten me: trips in the back of pickup trucks, the vacuum (the sound, the sharp smell, the way things disappear inside it), and anytime Max or Emmaline are in danger. That night, as the sheepdog cast a final red-eyed glance in my direction, its ears back and incisors gleaming, I added one more thing to the list.

Previously, I took great pride in knowing the name of every dog in the neighborhood. Names mean something: they are how we present ourselves to the world. Take Cosmo, for instance. Mom once explained that Cosmo means "of the universe"; then she pointed up at the sky, and Max got out his long metal tube that allows you to see the stars up close. It made me feel important, like I was part of something bigger than myself. I have intense sympathy for dogs named Muffin or Scooby or Biscuit. How can they hold their tails up? With the sheepdog, I chose to simply call it by its breed. I chose not to name my fear.

The sheepdog is normally trapped behind a wooden fence, but each Halloween it is let loose to greet the trick-or-treaters.

And I must face it.

Emmaline skips ahead of us, her light-up sneakers casting shadows on the sidewalk. I trot alongside Max, my leash limp in his hand. The evening is brisk but mild—"sweater weather," humans call it. A breeze shivers through my fur, carrying with it a variety of wonderful scents. Apple pie! Squirrels! Rotten leaves! Momentarily, I forget about the sheepdog and my embarrassing costume, letting myself revel in the smells, my tail whipping through the air. I press my nose to the ground, and almost immediately—what's this? Candy corn!

"Cosmo," Max says, gently shaking my leash. "Leave it. It'll give you a stomachache."

But I'm so overcome by the candy corn's smell, by its lovely symmetry against the pavement, that I make a second attempt. My tongue has almost scraped it from the ground when I'm pulled in another direction.

Max glances down at me, picking up the pace. "Sorry, Cosmo. I'll give you a cookie when we get home, okay?"

I trust that Max will keep his word, so I lower my head and trail him down a brick path, where two women are perched on a stoop, garbed in black dresses with pointy hats. Behind the glass front door, a Maltese named Cricket yaps itself hoarse. My patience for small breeds is limited. According to the Discovery Channel, which I watch frequently when Max and Emmaline are at school, all dogs are descendants of wolves. But looking at Cricket, who barely makes it to my knees, I question the truth of that research.

"Awww," one of the women coos, dropping a lollipop in Emmaline's plastic pumpkin. "What do we have here? A superhero and a giraffe?"

A giraffe! I knew it!

Max stares at his toes—and I nudge the palm of his hand, digging my nose inside it; I do this to remind him that I am here. Around some humans, Max refuses to speak, and his heartbeat pounds in his fingers.

"Oh my *goodness*," the second woman says, spotting me. "And a turtle! Cosmo, you're a *turtle*! Come here, boy, come here." She pats her lap, as if I'm supposed to jump on top of it. Apparently she has not heard about my arthritis. The last few years, my joints have gotten sore: a burning ache that I lick and lick. Still, out of a sense of neighborly duty, I partially oblige her, even though I feel—just slightly—like she is mocking me. Her fingers smell of those miniature sausages Mom wraps in pastry dough and pops in the oven on holidays. Last Christmas, I devoured seven when Dad left his tray unattended. I can still recall the way the sausages felt sliding down my throat: warm, salty, oblong. It was the fourth best day of my life.

"Getting many trick-or-treaters this year?" Dad asks the women, sticking his hands in the pockets of his jeans.

"Oh, loads!" the one scratching my ears answers. "We've had lots of ghosts, a few pirates, an avocado . . . And the night is still young!"

The expression doesn't add up. How can a night be young?

Old. Young. Usually I am good with ages. Emmaline

is five. Max is twelve. And I am thirteen—eighty-two in human years. In our neighborhood, there is only one dog older than me: a yellow Labrador named Peter, who manages with the help of a cart strapped to his hindquarters. I have heard rumors of the existence of doggy diapers, of pills that artificially prolong your life. I am uninterested in those options. But I also know that, as the eldest member of my family, I need to be there for them as long as I can, any way I can.

Good thing I have a whole lot of life left in me.

We depart from the stoop, kids giggling in the street, parents chasing them down with flashlights, and we repeat the process dozens of times: approaching the neighbors, begging for food. I've always found this interesting. When I beg underneath the dining-room table, my nose wedged between knees, the results vary. Sometimes Max passes me a corner of his sandwich, lets me lick the meaty juices from his plate. Other times, Dad scolds me with "No, *out,*" and I'm banished to the living room, where I chew self-pityingly on a rope toy. The rules are different for humans.

I am beginning to slow down, my breath more labored, when—*we're here.* In front of the sheepdog's house. My hackles stand up.

But where is the demon dog? I can't see it! I can't even smell it!

Max answers my whimpers. "What's wrong, Cosmo?"

What's *wrong*? The giraffe costume must be infecting him with its horrible giraffe power. Surely it's obvious: the sheepdog is plotting something!

Emmaline sucks in her breath and lets it all out. "I'm tired, Daddy." Her cape drags along the sidewalk, crisp leaves stuck to the bottom.

"You wanna go home?" Dad asks. "Your buckets are pretty full."

The sheepdog! Why is no one concerned about the sheepdog?

Max says, "I'm up for whatever Emmaline wants. I've got enough candy for, like, a year."

What's this? The three of them are turning to head for home. No! I plant my paws and refuse to budge. If the sheepdog is hatching a plan, it must be stopped.

Max tugs at my leash. "Cosmo, come on, please?"

No.

Dad says, "Cosmo, let's go."

No.

Emmaline rests her hands on my back. *"Cosmooooo."*

Eventually Dad takes the leash and pulls, slowly but hard, and I'm forced away from the sheepdog's

house, the windows glowing amber in the autumn night. *Wait. Wait!* In the final seconds, directly on its yard, I lift my leg and release a stream of urine. As a signal. As a warning. *I'm onto you.*

I depart, on edge but mostly satisfied.

Back at our house, as promised, I get a cookie, and Emmaline and Max divide up their candy on the living-room floor: piles for lollipops, piles for chocolate, piles for the candy no one likes. "Yuck," Emmaline says, tossing a box of raisins to the side. Her black curls whip back and forth as she shakes her head. "Yuck, yuck, *yuck.*"

I observe from my position on the couch, which is difficult to climb onto nowadays. Sometimes it takes several tries, several embarrassing topples. A long time ago, I was not allowed on furniture, which made little sense. Wasn't my dog bed constructed of similar materials? Why was I allowed on one, but forbidden to lie on the other? Eventually, Dad gave up his couch crusade, and the cushions began to form around the shape of my body. I've learned that perseverance is a powerful thing.

The TV is on in the background. A talking black cat parades across the screen. Why do cats always get to speak on TV? Where are all the talking dogs? The dog in the movie *Up* speaks, but only with a translation collar. Lassie, the most famous TV dog of all time, just barks. I'm puzzling over the inequity when the back door slams. It is incredibly loud, purposeful. And then the voices begin.

Mom growls in the kitchen, "David, did you *really*?"

"What?" Dad says.

"You were supposed to wait for me! I told you I'd be working late! I didn't even get to see the kids in their costumes . . ."

"They're still in their costumes."

"I mean out in the neighborhood, trick-or-treating. I was supposed to go with you, remember? Or did you conveniently just forget?"

"That's unfair. You were *late.*"

Mom throws up her hands. "I *told* you I was going to be late. That's why I asked you to wait for me!"

I don't like the way they're speaking to each other. From the couch, I give them a disapproving look. Can't they see Max and Emmaline are happy, that their voices are ruining it? Emmaline slowly crumples to the side, laying her head on the carpet next to the raisins, while Max tugs his knees to his chest.

"Let's just . . ." Dad says, "let's just get a picture, okay? That's what you want, right?"

"What I want? You don't *care* about what I want."

But we take the picture anyway, the five of us crowded by the fireplace, smiling at a small camera. After a few moments, a flash fills the room, and Max says quickly, "Okay, I guess I'm going to bed."

Mom glances at him hopefully. "You don't want to stay up a little bit? Watch *Halloweentown* with me?"

"I'm . . . I'm kinda tired."

"Oh," Mom says. "Sure, okay. Good night, sweetie."

"Night." He kisses Emmaline on the forehead. "Night, Em."

As I do every evening, I follow Max into his bedroom. Posters of the night sky stare down at us from the walls. There's also a large picture of Guy Bluford, the first African American in space. He flew four shuttle missions beginning in the early 1980s. I know this because Max shares things with me; being an astronaut is his dream.

Curling at the edge of his bed, I rest my head on my paws. Uneasiness crawls through me. Something is wrong. I've heard that dogs can sense hurricanes and tsunamis when they're still miles offshore. This is similar.

Max closes the door — and immediately bursts into tears.

Crying?

Max rarely cries. Only when he's fallen off his bike, or slipped on a patch of ice, or —

I don't have time to think about it. I just react, standing as quickly as I can, rushing toward him as his back slides against the wall, as he folds to the floor. I lick his face. His ears. His fingers. I wedge my head between his hands and rest my muzzle on his shoulder. Shaking, his arms wrap around me, and he whispers directly into my ear, "Never leave me, Cosmo. Never leave me, okay?"

Why would I leave? Why would I ever leave Max?

I nuzzle him deeper in response.

And we stay like that for a long, long time.

I was born a puppy, thirteen years ago in a garage near Myrtle Beach, South Carolina. I do not recall much about my early life, except cardboard boxes under my paws and the whines of my siblings, who always nudged me away from the food dish.

I also remember the day I met Mom and Dad. Back then, they were called Zora and David Walker.

It was one of those pale blue mornings in early spring, and the man who changed the cardboard boxes leaned into our pen, pointing a long finger at my front paws. "See here? He's pigeon-toed. I reckon all his sisters are show-dog quality, but him, I'll go half-price."

Zora peeked in. She had a round head of black curls and her eyes were kind. She smelled of things I could not yet name but would later identify as rosemary soap and apples.

I licked the back of her hand, half to say hello, half to determine its taste.

"He's so sweet," she cooed.

"You sure you don't want one of the females?" David asked. I looked up at him for the first time and immediately pegged him as part spaniel, fur floppy and brown against his white forehead. What he was crossed with, I did not know, but it was a breed that tapered his nose at the sides.

"I'm sure," Zora said.

I went home with them that day, to a ranch-style house in a quiet North Carolina neighborhood. Out of sheer nervousness, I threw up twice in the four-hour drive, and Zora cleaned me in the bathtub with warm water and that rosemary soap, whispering "Little Cosmo, everything's all right." And it was. Our first year was punctuated with cuddling Zora as her stomach grew bigger, learning a handful of commands, and appreciating the difference between carpet and grass—specifically, which was an appropriate place to relieve myself.

It wasn't long before Max arrived.

Three days after the delivery, David cradled Max in his arms and folded himself onto the living-room floor, right next to me. "You're a big brother now, Cosmo. You up to the job?"

Was I?

I sniffed Max's tiny face, perplexed. I had perhaps naively assumed that humans were born with a full body of fur and, as they aged, shed their outer layer. But—except for the wisps on his head—Max's brown skin was smooth and bare.

A big brother. The enormity of the responsibility hit me as Max slowly opened his eyes, and they were glassy and full of something that I can only describe as admiration. He was perfect. I loved him instantly.

Yes. Yes, I was up to it.

I conveyed this with a short but meaningful *woof.* David took one hand from Max and smoothed the crinkled fur on the back of my neck, something he had never really done. I saw it as a pact between us. I would protect Max, and David would love me in return. In those moments, we became a family.

There is a word I've learned in the twelve years since: *doggedly.* It means "with persistence and full effort." Humans attribute this to a dog's stubbornness—our refusal to give up chewy sticks, the way we freeze in the doorway when it rains. But really it's the way we love, with our whole hearts, no matter the circumstance.

I vowed to protect Max—and my family—doggedly, for the rest of my life.

The morning after Halloween, Max is awake early.
I hear him throw off the covers and tiptoe down the
hall to the bathroom, water rushing through pipes.

As a young dog, I loved mornings. I was a kid on
Christmas. I would spring up at the sound of movement, lick sleeping faces, bark at the back door—*out,
out, out!* And finally Dad would succumb to my will,
grumbling, "Okay, Cosmo, okay," and we'd romp
through the dewy grass, watching the sun split sideways over the neighborhood. Now I am slower. Even
my bones ache today.

I get up carefully, stretching my back legs, and
take a few measured steps off my plush bed, which

Mom has sprayed with a flowery mist. Humans are obsessive about animal smells—always trying to mask them with other scents that will never smell as rich or as good. My theory is this: because humans relieve themselves in bathrooms instead of in the great outdoors, they have little urine left to mark their territory. Flower sprays are a poor substitute.

More sounds: the toilet flushing, an alarm buzzing, Mom murmuring something.

Food. The thought does strike me. I pride myself on seldom succumbing to baser urges, but I find that—besides the opening and closing of the garage door—meals are the best indicators of time. My days are measured in segments, a series of events leading to Max leaving and returning from school. I dream of summer, when there is no leaving, and we spend long days by the lake, fetching sticks, grilling burgers, and diving off the dock into the water, our bodies weightless and free.

Mom peeks her head into Max's room, peering in my direction. "Morning."

My tail waves through the air, and I try to scramble over, slipping slightly on the hardwood, my nails tapping. I love how everyone in this family speaks to me—like I am human, too. Some dogs, their humans

merely issue a set of commands: *Sit! Stay! Go potty!* There's no conversation. There's no humanity.

Have *you* ever tried to poo on command? Not that easy, not that easy.

"Good boy," Mom says, crouching down and running her hands over the sides of my muzzle, which I'm told is almost completely white. "Yes, you're such a good dog. How did you sleep, huh?" She kisses the top of my head, and I trail her into the kitchen, where something lingers. Stress. Anxiety. Sadness. I bet humans don't know that emotions have specific scents, but for a few moments, they're all I can smell.

A food bowl appears, and I swiftly eat my kibble—followed by a spoonful of peanut butter. When Mom's back is turned, I sift the peanut butter over the roof of my mouth, clacking it loudly to extract the smooth, round vitamin, which I deposit covertly, deep into the crevice between the cabinets and the refrigerator. Emmaline waddles into the kitchen then, still in her footie pajamas, and Mom hurries her toward a bowl of Cheerios. Generally speaking, Emmaline and I are on the same feeding schedule.

Everything is rushed this morning, I notice. Everything happens too quickly. Max blows into the kitchen, his hair wet, and barely says goodbye before catching the large yellow bus. Dad grabs a leftover container of spaghetti from the refrigerator and leaves without a word. And Mom ushers me into the backyard with a wave of her hands; I wander around for a few moments, do my business, and am almost immediately called back inside. This disappoints me greatly, as there were several interesting smells that I wished to explore: something rotting underneath a pile of leaves, smoke in the air, a yellow stain in the grass that might be my own but perhaps not.

I'm starting to feel anxious myself.

Later Mom says, "Be a good boy today, okay, Cosmo?" and closes the front door, Emmaline in tow. Max has left the TV on for me in the study, for which I am always grateful. Days without TV are like days without oxygen; I am forced to wander aimlessly around the house, the only sounds my claws clicking against the floor and the occasional ring of the phone. I sleep to pass the time and awake groggy, determined to entertain myself with something, anything. Chew toys often lose their appeal after the first week. I have no cat to play with. The bathroom doors remain closed following that first instance, many years ago, when I discovered the joy of toilet paper, unrolling sheet after sheet in frenzied merriment. Television is my saving grace.

Max rotates between several channels to give me variety. The news is my least favorite. I do not see how humans stand it, or, frankly, how humans stand one another; sometimes it seems like the world is full of bad people doing bad things. (My family is an exception, of course.) The Discovery Channel is much more to my liking: tales of the Alaskan wilderness, survival in extreme environments, and fish bigger than me! But I must admit that my absolute favorite channel is Turner Classic Movies.

That is where I first discovered *Grease.*

It was a Friday night in late winter, and my family had ordered pizza from the restaurant next to the grocery store: three large pies with pepperoni, sausage, and extra cheese. The five of us settled into the study, where I strategically positioned myself as close to the pizzas as possible, earning several crusts for my efforts and unparalleled stealth.

"Oh, go back, that channel!" Mom suddenly said.

"This?" Max said.

"Yes! I haven't seen *Grease* for so long. Trust me, you'll like it."

And I did. I liked it very, very much.

Grease is a cinematic masterpiece with wonderful songs, including "You're the One That I Want" and

"We Go Together." No dogs grace the screen, but I do not hold that against it, because it has everything I love about people: passion, dance moves, and the resilience of the human heart. *Nothing* about humans is as complex as their hearts; I learned that from Sandy and Danny, the main characters in *Grease,* who fall apart before falling back together. I came away from my first viewing with an unmistakable sense of lightness. I tried not to act too excited, too changed, but before bed, I shoved my nose into my water dish and snorted several times, watching the liquid burble and fly—which was perhaps a clear indication that I was thoroughly and unexpectedly happy. That night, I fell asleep quickly. And I dreamed of dancing.

In some ways, I have never truly stopped.

Jealousy is not in my nature. However, I've known dogs who are incredibly frustrated by their limitations — by comparing themselves to humans. *It is not your fault,* I try to tell them, *that you have no thumbs to lift the TV remote, no skillful tongue to speak.* And after all, dogs have many advantages over people.

Case in point: I have never seen a human on all fours, pressing his face to the ground, attempting to track a scent. Their noses are remarkably inferior to ours. I am no bloodhound, but I would recognize Max's smell anywhere; I could follow the scent of his footprints through a forest scattered with leaves. If you need more evidence, please also consider the book

To Kill a Mockingbird, which Max read last summer for school. No dog would have to consult a manual for such a simple task! To be clear, I have never killed a mockingbird, but for the sake of argument, it would be almost insultingly easy: track smell, put bird in mouth, close mouth.

Dogs are also superior in the following ways: We acknowledge danger when humans won't—their capacity for denial is much, much greater. We forgive readily and often. And we do not feel one emotion while displaying another; take, for example, the prevalence of humans claiming "I'm fine," when they are not fine at all.

I am only envious of people in two respects.

First, human families stick together forever, through ups and downs, highs and lows, because love binds them. I feel as much a part of the Walker family as Emmaline and Max . . . and yet I do wish I still knew my sisters. I wish I knew my mother; I remember so little of her.

And second, dancing.

For all their faults, humans can dance.

In the early years, Mom and Dad would switch on jazz music and dance barefoot in the kitchen. They'd intertwine their hands and sway side to side, turning

now and then, while I looked on in astonishment. How could they spin so smoothly? How could they dip like that? As a dog, my initial reaction was to separate them; in the wild, few animals weave together without a fight. So I wiggled between legs, knocked into knees, trampled on toes.

Still, they danced.

Sometimes Mom and Dad would disappear for long stretches of night, stumbling home with tired feet. "You should've seen us," they'd say, describing every detail: the songs, the atmosphere, the way they moved.

It wasn't until Emmaline and Max arrived that something finally clicked, and I understood deeply for the first time—how dancing is an extension of the soul. Although I am prone to exaggeration, I must say, without hyperbole or embellishment: dance nights transformed my family. Mom and Dad began staying in, rolling up the living-room rug, and the four of them jumped together and spun together and raised their hands together, music thumping through the house. Everywhere else, Max was shy, but in the living room he zigzagged, jiggled, skipped.

Him—this was *him*!

"Cosmo," he always called to me, right in the middle of the dance, "come!"

In response, I'd edge backward, slinking quietly onto the sofa. When I used to run (chasing a tennis ball in the dog park, breaking free from the yard to rush after Max's school bus), I felt fluid and infinite, as if I were merely slipping through the sky. That is the closest I've come to achieving what I witnessed on dance nights, what I saw in *Grease*. I know my limitations. Especially now, with my joints and my bones, I will never stand for prolonged periods on my back legs, spinning in elegant circles and hopping effortlessly from place to place.

All I can do is dream. And dream, I do.

Early November passes quickly, and for a few glorious weeks, it's as if the events of Halloween never occurred. The sad smell evaporates from the kitchen. Mom and Dad do not raise their voices. And Max is busy constructing a rocket for the science fair; it will shoot two hundred feet into the sky, right into the stars he loves so much. The weather is surprisingly warm, and Emmaline and I spend the afternoons jumping into pile after pile of autumn leaves, laughing ourselves silly. On the weekends, Dad cooks breakfast—banana pancakes, fried eggs, bacon—and Max sneaks me bits and pieces, which I gobble with enthusiasm.

Occasionally, I save a half strip of bacon, hiding it behind the couch for a rainy day, because you never know when rainy days will come.

The evening before Thanksgiving, I sense a shift. That hurricane feeling, like something shaky is on the horizon. It begins at the dining-room table, where Emmaline and Max are tracing their hands, assembling construction-paper turkeys, and I have plopped my head on Max's lap, desperately hoping that he'll pay attention to me.

"Subtle," he says, peering down with a smile. Abandoning the turkey (*take that, stupid bird!*), he's about to run his hands over the coarse fur on my back—but he's interrupted when Mom bursts through the back door, dropping ten plastic bags of groceries on the table with a massive *thunk.*

"David!" she yells.

Dad rushes in from the study, his hair ruffled. "What?"

"Why'd I just get a call from your mother that she and Steve are coming to Thanksgiving?"

"Grandma and Grandpa are coming?" Emmaline pipes in, happy and oblivious.

Max lays a hand over her hand and shakes his head. Human communication is largely nonverbal,

which is perhaps part of the reason I feel so close to them: I rely on gestures, too.

"I invited them," Dad says, voice tight. "I'm allowed to do that, right?"

"Of course you are. But you said that you weren't, and I only bought food for four people . . ."

"Then we'll go out and get some more."

"It's the principle of it," Mom says. "And the store's a zoo."

"Fine," Dad says, thrusting out his hand. "I'll go. Give me the keys."

"No, I'll —"

"*I'll* go."

I've learned that intonation has meaning. Simple words turn sour, depending on the way you say them.

Max tugs softly at my collar, Emmaline's little hand grasping his. The three of us head as silently as possible to his bedroom. He shuts the door.

Normally I cannot make the leap from the ground onto the bed, and Max isn't strong enough to lift me. According to the vet, I am ninety-four pounds— overweight for a dog of my breed. On special occasions, though, Max grabs a set of small stairs. Now his arms guide my back legs up the steps as I slide into a bundle of bedding.

"Here we go," he says. "That's it."

And suddenly, I've almost forgotten Mom and Dad's fight in the kitchen—because look at me! Look at me, curled in this duvet, practically on top of the world! My tail wags uncontrollably.

Emmaline rolls onto the bed, too, settling her head between my front paws. "Cosmo," she says quietly, peering up at my jowls, "you look funny from below." I note our positioning and see an opportunity to lick her nostrils, so I do. They're warm and dry under my tongue. This upsets me: Emmaline will never know the perfect joy of running a wet nose through fresh-cut grass, of lifting a cold snout to the wind.

She squeals, wiggling away from me.

In the corner of the room, Max grabs his laptop. Over the past few years, I've heard this word more and more, because Max is always looking at pictures of stars on the screen. Sometimes he points to the glowing dots and tells me names like Orion and Canis Major, and I always sit very, very still, so that I may listen with my ears and my heart. Now he sets up the laptop for us to view, and Emmaline stretches out her feet. There are blue socks halfway up her ankles.

"Are those clouds?" she asks, pointing to several swirls on the screen.

"Yeah," Max says softly. "From above. It's what the astronauts see on the International Space Station."

In the kitchen, Mom's and Dad's voices climb, making me so uneasy that I need to urinate. This always happens when I am anxious, even if I've just been outside. My accidents in the house are few and far between, but those little puddles are a great source of embarrassment and shame. I focus on other things: the warmth of the blankets, the whirl of the ceiling fan, and the comforting scent of Max's room, which smells of peppermint and grass and him. I think about spaghetti dinners with extra spaghetti—and family dance nights, even though they don't happen anymore.

Max sighs. Emmaline shuffles over to rest her head on his shoulder.

I hold my urine.

It's the least I can do for them.

The morning of Thanksgiving is cloudy with rain.
Under the shield of a massive umbrella, Max and I
take a quick walk through the neighborhood so I may
relieve myself before Grandma and Grandpa arrive.
We tread through sidewalk puddles, the aroma of turkey all around.

Turkey is my favorite, though I am rarely con-
sulted about holiday meals. At Thanksgiving, Easter,
and Christmas, the rules for me are very simple: Don't
bark too much. Don't eat anything I'm not offered. If
we're traveling and there is a cat, don't taunt the cat.
Max is the only one who cares about my menu prefer-
ences. He can even name the holiday foods I love most:

turkey thigh (juicy, meaty, delicious), turkey giblets (very chewy, very nice), and those miniature sausages wrapped in pastry.

Just thinking about food, my mouth begins to water. But I stroll on, paws flicking, until we enter a cluster of pine trees. Max tugs on my leash, stopping me, the ground soft and squelching beneath us.

"Can I tell you a secret?" he asks, one hand in his pocket. I hope the secret is *I have a cookie hidden in the fabric of my jeans,* so I tell him, *Always.* He shifts from foot to foot, his sneakers digging deeper into the pine needles. The world suddenly feels very quiet—only our breath and the mud and the rain. My ears perk, head tilting.

Max says it in a burst: "I'd skip Thanksgiving this year if I could."

I try to work out the meaning of his words. Who'd want to skip Thanksgiving, especially when turkey is involved? *The sausages, Max!* Surely he remembers the sausages!

"It's just . . ." he says, trailing off. "It's just that everything seems to get worse when Mom and Dad are pretending to be happy in front of other people. Because I don't think they're very happy. Not really."

When he explains it that way, I begin to understand.

I shove my nose into his palm, over and over, to say, *I'm here.* If I could speak words, I'd tell him about Mom and Dad dancing all those years ago, about the bare feet and the twirling, the jazz music in the kitchen. I'd tell him that I miss our dance nights, too. Although I never participated with my paws or my legs, I loved watching my family, how they glided and spun, their souls on full display. And Max, my Max—he always looked so unafraid. On those nights, we would have doughy pizza and open all the windows; we'd stay up until the squirrels fell asleep and the buzzing bugs crawled from their underground holes.

My family hasn't danced like that for a while, longer than I'd like to admit. Now Mom and Dad fight about human things that matter so little. They argue about the garbage cans and the leaky pipe in the bathroom and "bills," though I cannot see—not for the life of me—how the mouths of ducks have anything to do with my family. Ducks in general are very boring.

Max toes the mud with the tip of his sneaker, as if a squeaky toy is hidden just below the surface. "You probably don't know this," he says, "but Uncle Reggie—you remember him? He was supposed to make it for Thanksgiving, but he won't be back for another couple of days, and Mom's really sad about it. She didn't tell me, but I know she is. I heard her crying. Again."

This is news to me. Usually I'm very good about keeping track of our family—our plans, our emotions. But occasionally the ring of our doorbell surprises me, and strange shoes appear on the mat, socks bundled up inside. You can tell a lot about a person from the scent of their socks: eating habits, bathing habits, if they are happy or stressed. I never forget a sock smell. I haven't seen Mom's brother, Uncle Reggie, since I was a puppy, but his smell is still there, buried deep within me. Earth and oats. Hamburger on his finger-tips. Those lotions that humans rub all over, to make themselves shiny and smooth.

I remember his hair, too. Twisted into long dark strands that I nipped, because I was young and didn't know any better. He laughed like something was bouncing in his belly—then let me nibble on the ends of his hair. "This one's gonna be a handful," he told Mom. There must be bulldog somewhere in his lineage: his smile was wide and kind.

"Make sure you raise him well," he said.

And Mom said, "We will."

The next day Uncle Reggie disappeared with his shoes and his socks. Sometimes I still hear his voice coming out of objects in the house (Max's laptop, the telephone that rings angrily in the living room), and I've always wondered if this is my imagination. Did I love his smell so much that I summoned the sound of him?

"Anyway," Max says, shaking his head. Rain splats on the umbrella. "We should probably get back. Go potty, Cosmo. Please."

Our conversation shouldn't end—not here. Max needs to talk; I sense this very clearly. But I also feel a powerful responsibility when it comes to going potty in the woods. Choosing a place to squat requires instinct and observation, talent and bravery. If I come across a section of earth that the sheepdog has marked, then I must mark it as well to keep the evil at bay.

The demon dog lurks everywhere.

Checking over my shoulder, I relieve myself safely by the base of a tree, and Max and I begin trotting toward home. He starts whistling the theme song from *Star Wars,* a series of films that I enjoy, despite its lack of dogs. I identify strongly with Chewbacca, the hairiest character, whose fur is close in texture to mine.

In the driveway, Max stops whistling.

Grandma and Grandpa's car is parked underneath our basketball hoop.

Although Emmaline and Max love Dad's parents, I think they smell like onions: stinging and sharp. I trust my gut and my nose about these things. Both have always told me to be wary of Grandma and Grandma, especially after last Christmas, when Grandpa forced me outside right before dinner. "Go on," he said, poking me with his knee. "The kitchen's no place for dogs."

Then he closed the door in my face.

The sky went dark, and I spent an hour — or maybe it was five — circling the swing set in the frigid backyard. I also dug a deep, deep hole by the recycling bins. It was so bottomless that I began to feel dizzy, disoriented, and thought very briefly about eating the growing pile of dirt by my paws. I didn't. As a puppy, I learned the hard way: a belly full of dirt will never improve your mood.

"Well," Max says now, breathing stiffly with his chest. I watch it rise up and down. "Here we go."

Inside, we dry off by the front door. I swipe my paws on the mat, as I've been taught to do, and shake slightly, beads of rain rocketing off my fur.

Grandma rushes up to us, hugging Max tightly. "There's my boy! Oh, you've *grown*! I just can't keep up with you!"

Max squirms, anxiety wafting from him. His throat bobs—and I recognize the familiar signs: the sweat on his palms, the quickening of his heart. In this way, I believe we are similar. I understand the stress that comes from not being able to speak when you want to, how your tongue fills your mouth but refuses to move in the right ways.

"Happy Thanksgiving," he murmurs, and it's not the Max voice, the strong voice he shares with me. It's the one he uses for strangers and the mailman and young humans who, if he were a dog, would bristle the back of his neck.

"Turkey day!" Grandma shouts in return. "I packed my stretch jeans!"

Grandma and Grandpa are what humans call "Floridians." I haven't figured out the meaning of this, but I assume it has to do with the big, fluffy sweaters they always wear at holidays. The sweaters are scarily close to the sheepdog's fur. You have to wonder: What's beneath the fluff? What are they hiding?

Grandma stoops to pat my head. "Hellooooo, cute

puppy, hi, hi, how are youuuuu today? Ooooo, you're a bit wet and smelly, aren't you?"

Why do some humans speak to dogs like this, words stretched out, as if we can't really understand?

At least she recognizes that I smell fantastic.

"I brought you a special treat!" she continues. "Yes, I did!" From the depths of her sweater, Grandma pulls out a biscuit the color of sand, and I already know it will be chalky and flavorless. She zooms it toward my mouth. When I don't immediately open up, she frowns. "You don't want the cookie?"

I take the cookie.

For the family, I take the cookie. How would it look if I didn't?

The three of us pad our way into the living room, where tiny men in helmets are running around on TV. Dad and Grandpa are busy yelling at them as scents drift from the kitchen: Turkey juices! Turkey thighs! Turkey everything! I can feel tendrils of drool escaping the corners of my lips. During a break in the football game, Mom ushers Max and Emmaline into their bed-rooms to put on "nice clothes," and I follow Dad into the kitchen, my nails clacking on the linoleum, my excitement soaring.

"Want a little bit?" Dad asks. He removes a small piece of turkey leg from the tray and feeds it to me in his open palm. I gobble it down, leaving a long strand of slobber.

Behind me, Grandpa snaps, "Oh, don't waste that good food on the dog!"

I take offense to this on a variety of levels. Dogs appreciate food *more* than humans (the level of saltiness, its shape, the texture in our mouths). "The dog" is also tremendously rude. My name is Cosmo.

"It's only a tiny amount," Dad says, swiping his slobbery hand on a dishcloth.

Grandma slides into the kitchen next to Grandpa. They both smell tense, and they fidget like the birds in the trees. Grandma grabs a carrot stick from the vegetable tray and chomps—but not hard enough for extra pieces to drop to the ground. *I am here,* I tell her. *If you offered me a carrot, I wouldn't say no.*

Instead, she asks Dad, "Have you given any more thought to what we talked about?"

Dad bristles. "Jeez, not now. It's Thanksgiving."

"I'm just telling you, the longer this thing goes on, the worse it'll get. You need to think of the kids."

"I *am* thinking of the kids," Dad says. "That's why it's so hard." There's something angry in his eyes, like

he just caught Grandma peeing on the rug. "Let's not talk about it in front of —"

"Who?" Grandpa says, stepping in. "The dog? All he hears is *blah, blah, blah, Cosmo, blah, blah, blah.*"

For a second, I am dumbfounded: to be insulted so openly, in my own home!

"I meant Zora and the kids," Dad says in a hushed voice. "In the other room."

Grandma takes a final bite of the carrot stick, offering me none. "Okay. But eventually you're going to have to make a decision. No getting around it."

With that, they all begin to busy themselves in the kitchen. I puzzle over Grandma's words as pots clatter. Utensils clink. Garlic sizzles in a pan. When the scents become so strong that I begin sneezing, Emmaline emerges from the hallway in a polka-dotted outfit, the cape from Halloween slung over her shoulders.

"Ta-da!" she says, spinning, brown skin glittering in the light.

Max comes up behind her and shrugs. "She insisted on wearing it."

Dad smiles. It doesn't reach his eyes. "Very nice. You look like Wonder Woman." He turns to Max. "Wanna help with the turkey, big guy?"

"Um," Max says, "okay."

From my position on the floor, I can see everything. Dad, carving the rest of the turkey and arranging it on a metal tray. Grandma, trying to make more space on the countertop. Max, grabbing the turkey tray with "I've got it. Don't worry." But the tray is too hot, so he sets it down on the kitchen stool—the one Emmaline uses to reach the sink. He moves to grab a pair of oven mitts. In those seconds, all the possibilities sparkle before me. The turkey is just there. There and waiting.

I am too eager.

I feel myself losing control.

Despite my bad hips, I clamor forward, sinking my canine teeth into a drumstick. Time seems to stop. I have the dreaded sense that I've miscalculated something: the force of my bite, the way I've shoved my nose into the bird. The stool wobbles. The tray wobbles. And in slow motion, the whole thing topples onto the linoleum, spraying turkey guts and juice and soggy carrots in a delicious arc.

I'm caught between feelings of terror and absolute joy. There is *turkey* on the *floor*! I dart toward the splattered pieces, shoving as much in my mouth as quickly as I possibly can. Muffled voices float above me:

"What the—?"

"Cosmo!"

"*Nooo!*"

But in this space, in this moment, it's just the tur-key and me, and I want to *conquer* it. I want to *live inside* it. The hot rush fills my throat. I eat and gag and eat and gag until I feel a sharp tug on my col-lar, dragging me back. That's when I realize what I've done. Dad stares down at me with an intense look of disappointment. Grandma clutches her hands to her chest. But Max jumps in to defend me.

"It's not his fault!" he says. "He was probably really hungry! It was my fault. I . . . I'm sorry. The tray . . . Don't be mad."

"Oh my goodness," Mom says, rushing into the kitchen. "What happened?" She glances at me, slob-ber and turkey grease coating my mouth.

Dad says, "What does it look like?"

Mom blinks. "Okay, it's fine, we'll just . . . Order a main dish? I'm sure something's open."

"On *Thanksgiving*?" Dad snaps.

"*Yes,*" Mom snaps back.

"Don't fight," Max says, peering down at the tur-key, although he is most likely speaking to Mom and Dad. "Please, don't fight."

I cower, ashamed. So little is expected from me

on holidays, and I've broken a golden rule: don't eat food unless it is offered. I stare at the wreckage by my paws, wondering if this is all a bad dream.

Grandpa says, "And *that's* why you don't let dogs in the kitchen."

In the following minutes, Max cleans up my mess with rolls and rolls of paper towels. Mom orders pizza with "Hi? Are you open? Phew. Wonderful." And Emmaline sets up the construction paper turkeys on the table. When the pizza arrives, I banish myself—staying far, far away from the cheesy smell. Guilt—and turkey—weigh heavily in my stomach.

It is only later that Max and I speak again.

On the front porch, I shove my snout into the crook of his arm, my tail hanging. There is a piece of pumpkin pie on his lap, which I don't move to lick. We're alone, the two of us, under an autumn night full of stars.

"Hey, boy," he says, peering up at the sky.

Max once told me that he loves the sky the way I love tennis balls, and perhaps this is true. A ball is never *just* a ball: it's the smell, the bounce, the memories. It's camping trips and barbeques, winters and summers, Max and I playing fetch in dewy fields. "Just like that," he said. "Your tennis ball is my sky." Then he stroked my ears and explained that the universe is

expanding, that a great scientist named Carl Sagan sent a golden record into space. "There are loads of pictures on it," Max said, "plus sounds of Earth, like traffic, the ocean, whales."

And dogs? I wanted to ask him. *What about dogs?*

Max lowers his gaze toward me now, sighing deeply. "I know you didn't mean it, with the turkey." He pauses. "Well, I know you *meant* it, but if I were a golden retriever, I probably would have done the same thing."

If he were a golden retriever? Does he consider that a possibility, as I do with being human? I imagine myself catching balls skillfully, with my hands instead of my mouth. I would read books and understand all the words. I would be kind and gentle.

"And I'm sorry that people got upset with you," Max says. "Everyone's really stressed out, because I think Mom and Dad might be . . . They might be . . ." He loses his words, and I nudge him to say it's all right. Take your time. I have all the time in the world.

Moonlight creeps along the porch, lighting up the sidewalk and beyond. That strange pumpkin looks sad on the lawn, hollowed and drooping. There are ants in it, crawling in and out of the holes, and I would like to eat them, if I could. I'd like to chase them with my nose to the earth, scooping them up one by one.

"They might be getting a divorce," Max finally finishes, voice breaking. "Mom was talking on the phone the other day, when she thought I couldn't hear, and she said it, actually said the word. *Divorce.*"

He brings the heels of his hands to his eyes, shuddering. His shoulders shake. I have never smelled him like this, so angry and worried and scared. In the silence that engulfs us, I'm too bewildered to move. I've heard the word *divorce,* but always in movies, never in real life, never about our family.

Now someone is anxiously panting—and I realize with a start: *It's me.* I pant harder, harder, until it feels like my breath is faster than I can catch. In the old days, after our dance nights, my family would have sleepovers on the living-room floor. Does Max remember that? There were graham crackers and sleeping bags full of stuffing. There were socks taken off and put back on hours later, when the temperature dipped and the moon rose.

"Cosmo?" Max asks, pressing a hand to my bib. "Hey, it's okay. Slow down, boy. Slow down. All that turkey's probably catching up with you."

But it isn't the turkey. It isn't.

"I just wish I knew what was going to happen," he says after a long pause, after my panting slows. "Or if it's going to happen. All I know is I want us to stay together. We *have* to stay together. You and me."

I whimper from a deep place.

Because it never occurred to me, in any universe, that we wouldn't.

Grandma and Grandpa hang around for two more days, much to my disappointment. The whole house begins to reek of them. At night, they powder themselves with many bath products and wear slippers that Grandpa yanks from my view. "*Not* for dogs," he grunts at me, although his footwear is actually very dull. I have no interest in slippers.

Over a breakfast of crispy flakes and milk, I also hear Grandma and Grandpa talking about the sheepdog—how they pet it on their morning walk, how friendly it was. Friendly! Can you imagine?

To avoid them, I spend a good deal of time on the porch with Max, watching the last leaves float down from the trees. Whenever Max scoots closer to me, his fingers falling into my fur, I think about the possibility of our separation. "I've seen it happen," he explains in whispers, "with a kid at my school. His parents got divorced, so he went to live with his mom—and his dad got custody of their dog. I think that's how it works, a lot of the time. The mom gets the kids, but the dad still needs someone around, because he doesn't want to be lonely. And it isn't fair. It just isn't right. Grown-ups can do what they want, but why do *kids* have to get divorced from our best friends?"

The idea of Max staying with Mom, and me going with Dad, roils my stomach. Humans have always described Max and me as inseparable: so thoroughly connected that sometimes I don't know where he stops and I begin. We like the same brand of hot dogs. We watch the same TV programs. We are both interested in stars.

It's a very good thing that only one of us has body fur. Otherwise, it might be difficult to tell us apart.

Besides school and the occasional vacation, when I go off to doggy day care and spend my days lounging in foreign grass, Max and I have only been separated once, in Sawyer Park. He was rushing up and down the big blue slide as I barked from near the swings, and

Mom turned her head for *just* a second. It happened in one swish of my tail: the sheepdog crested the hill. An evil genius—I cannot deny it. Because in the next moment, Max was gone. To this day, I still don't know how the sheepdog managed to summon him past the jungle gym. But I remember Mom clutching her hands in her hair, and the pit of fear in my chest: heavy, like dirt. She untied my leash and I bolted. I was young then. I could run. And I didn't stop running until I found Max, by the ice-cream stand, a strawberry cone already dripping down his arm.

On the porch, for the first time, I almost wish that I were human, because humans can deny. A person could convince themselves that Mom and Dad's fighting will fade, that love binds all families in the end. But a dog—a dog will never smell something unpleasant and deny that it stinks.

Even so, it's difficult to wrap my mind around it. If Mom and Dad divorced, Max and I might end up in separate houses. How will I wake him up in the morning, then, tickling him with my whiskers? And Emmaline! Who will guard her chalk in the driveway as she rubs lines on the ground? What about family picnics, with miniature cheeses and peanut butter sandwiches that are so pleasing to chew, and picnic blankets that we lounge on, our bellies to the sky?

Once, the five of us traveled to a farm where I discovered horses, and creatures that are not horses, and smells consumed the air. Max, Emmaline, and I stood by a fence, watching grasshoppers flit through the pasture. Because I was quick, and stubborn when I wanted to be, I broke through the fence—bounding after the bugs with enormous leaps, Max and Emmaline on my tail. We have never laughed so hard, not even on dance nights.

I cannot live in one house, Emmaline and Max in another. I cannot be in the fields or the backyard or the cul-de-sac without them.

By Sunday morning, the ache in my stomach has grown into a hard, round ball. There are waffles, and we eat them slowly with the Weather Channel on in the background. "Good traveling conditions," Grandpa says. "Plenty of sun."

I'm just glad they're going home.

My tail flicks back and forth as we watch their car sputter into the distance. In the yard, Max leans down to pat the side of my belly. He's wearing the T-shirt that smells most like him. It's blue and yellow. Those are my favorite colors, because I can see them—so bright and so clear.

"Hey, Cosmo," he says. "Want to go for a car ride?"

I peer up at him, at the hair that curls over his bare ears, at his fantastically long arms that can reach for things like silverware and cookies, in ways that mine never will. And I tell him, *Yes, so much yes,* even though I have no idea where we're going. Car rides almost always lead to good things. And we could use good things.

Mom hurriedly unlocks the minivan and helps Max lift me inside. Our minivan is stunning: crumbs at the bottom of cup holders, shards of chips wedged between seats, and plenty of room—when the mood strikes me—to climb into the driver's seat while Mom is at the wheel. She loves this, too. We laugh and scream, the car swerving so wonderfully on the highway.

"I'm kind of nervous," Max says in the back, strapping on his seat belt and leaning his weight against me. I know my responsibility: I am there to hold him up.

"It's okay to be nervous," Mom says. I notice that her hair is tucked beneath a head wrap, the one she wore all the time when we were younger. It is speckled with stars. "You haven't spent that much time with him—mostly just on the phone. What were you . . . eight? Eight years old when you saw him last? Christmas or Thanksgiving, down in Florida."

"Yeah, eight," Max says, biting his lip. "What if he doesn't like me anymore?"

"Don't be silly. He *loves* you, always."

I rest my jaw on the windowsill as we travel down smooth roads, parking eventually in a crowded lot, the pavement cool under my paws. My first guess is *grocery store,* but why is Max telling me to follow him inside? I stick close to his heels, marveling at the sounds: humans calling to one another, horns beeping, glass doors sliding. Finally, I figure it out: we're at the airport, a place I've seen frequently on TV. Somehow I pictured it quieter, with a greater variety of suitcases.

Suitcases terrify me—even the idea of them. Large, boxy objects with unlimited space, they eat your possessions, then spit them back out. They stalk your family, trailing menacingly behind them. And when they're closed, who knows what's inside? Could be anything! Dad has a particularly frightening wheelie bag, and on occasion I've tried to crouch beside it. To test myself. To face my fear of the unknown. But I always abandon this pursuit: there are only so many ways that I can be brave.

Wait. The airport. Hackles standing, I realize something: Is it happening now? Am I leaving Max? Is Max leaving me? Horrified, I plant my feet and lock my legs, so stiff that Max has to drag me softly across the slick, slick floors.

"Come on," he says. "There's no reason to be scared."

And I believe him. I try to believe him. He's never lied to me before.

A little bit ahead of us, Mom is carrying large balloons with strings that twist up her arm. "Yoo-hoo!" she calls suddenly, waving a hand in the air. She often summons me this way, and for a moment, I'm confused. I'm already here! *Here I am!* But then I see a man, feet moving faster and faster toward us, his boots squeaking against the tile. He drops his rucksack and wraps his arms around Mom, who holds him tightly and whimpers for a long time. I wonder if he's hugging her too strongly in return, and if I should investigate. So I tug at the leash in Max's hands, sniffing the stranger, who—

Is *not* a stranger!

"Hello there, old friend," Uncle Reggie says, smiling that bulldog smile. He looks so much like Mom, with his smooth brown skin, his face warm and kind. When he kneels to kiss the crown of my head, it's as if no time has passed at all, as if I am still a puppy. My tail thumps on the floor. This man! You have no idea how magnificent he is, even though his head is bare, and I can no longer nip at the strands of him.

"You remember me?" he asks, laughing.

Of course! He smells the same. His *eyes* are the same: big and deep, and crinkly when he grins. I hold his gaze. From what I've seen on Turner Classic Movies, humans value direct contact. Eyes, they believe, are windows to the soul. And Uncle Reggie has a brilliant soul.

With another gentle pat, he stands and hugs Max. "Hey, champ."

"Hi," Max murmurs, sinking into Uncle Reggie's arms.

"Thanks for coming with your mom. I'm really sorry that I missed Thanksgiving—I'm sure it was fun." Pulling back from the hug, he grabs his rucksack, scoops through it, and retrieves a glossy piece of paper. "Hope you don't mind, but I got something for you."

"Whoa," Max says, taking the gift. His voice doesn't even creak. "This is . . . Wow. Thank you. It's *signed*?"

"Yep," Uncle Reggie says, tapping the picture. "This guy stopped by the base, and I told him all about you. Said my nephew wanted to be an astronaut, just like him." He rubs Max's head for a second, as he did with mine. "Man, it's good to see you again."

The excitement continues on the way home, when we stop at Max's favorite roadside restaurant. You would not believe what I discover! A hamburger patty, half-hidden in the grass. I chew it as silently as possible underneath the picnic table.

"What's that in your mouth?" Mom says.

"Oh, it's nothing," Uncle Reggie answers for me.

And I know that he knows. I know we have a secret.

Late that evening, after Max heads to bed, Uncle Reggie settles into the cushions on the couch. A slice of turkey bacon is buried beneath one—I just can't remember which—and I wonder if he will find it in the night. *With you,* I think, *I will share.*

This time of night, I hate leaving Max's room. But sometimes I become incredibly thirsty, my mouth so prickly and so dry, that I have no choice. I go in search of my water dish, lapping the liquid with quiet strokes. I take great care not to make too much noise, not to disturb anyone before sleep. My humans are always anxious about bedtime. There's rushing around and splashing, Emmaline in and out of the bath. Dad packs his workbag for the morning and fusses over tomorrow's lunch: Will he have spaghetti or chicken, chicken or spaghetti? And Max reads a book to soothe himself, although sometimes it takes him many hours to drift off. His nose twitches in his sleep.

The tags on my collar jingle as I take another step. By the couch, Uncle Reggie turns around — and jingles, too. Dog tags hang over his shirt, shining in the lamplight. This stuns me. A human with dog tags! Just when I thought I'd seen it all!

"So I guess I'm not the last one up," he says, smiling. "It's okay. Come on over here. Don't be shy."

I close the gap between us, his hands rubbing the sides of my head. He wipes the water droplets from my muzzle and touches my nose with his. I can smell the sadness on him.

He smells like our kitchen.

"You must see it all," he says. "By now, I bet you know them better than I do."

The refrigerator hums in the background. Somewhere in the house, floorboards creak. I can make out the voices: Mom and Dad fighting quietly in their bedroom closet, so no other humans can hear. But I can hear.

I hear everything.

"Protect their hearts," Uncle Reggie finally whispers to me. "Promise that you'll protect their hearts."

Every once in a while, I have an itch that I can't
scratch. Now that I am old, my legs won't bend the way
they used to, and my skin prickles with such intensity
that all I can do is shake. Whenever Max sees this,
he just knows: "Where's it itch? Here? Or here?" He'll
scratch along my body with his perfect human fingers,
until he finds the spot.

I would like to be that for him, always. Long ago, I
promised to love Max doggedly. Whatever he needed,
that's what I planned to give. And throughout the
years, I have given all that I have: when he's sick,
never leaving his side; when he's upset, bringing him
my favorite toys; when he's full of energy, keeping up

with him, traveling step for step through the neighbor-hood on cool autumn days. But I have been failing him lately. He has an itch, and I can't scratch it. Long ago, I could've run circles around him, could've distracted him from the scents in the kitchen: stress, anger, sad-ness. Now I sleep a good deal of the day, and dropping a chew toy by his feet only goes so far.

That night, I toss and turn on my plush bed, listening to the crickets and replaying Uncle Reg-gie's words. I wonder if his nose is strong, if he smells everything I smell. The air in our house has become deeply worrying; does he sense it, too? It feels stiff. Even my kibble tastes of cardboard. No matter how much I roll it around in my mouth, I can't extract any flavor from it. If I were human, I might blame this on the change in the weather—it's getting colder—but I know that the real shift is within us.

The next morning, Max rises early and brushes his teeth, which is always so impressive. (He never once gives into temptation and eats the toothbrush.) I study the lines of his pajamas, the careful way he combs his hair. I love everything about him. It's incon-ceivable, the idea of us apart.

"You look like you're thinking deep thoughts," he says to me, and I am.

Outside, we wait for the large yellow bus, my tail brushing through the dewy grass. Max rests his hand on my head and sighs. He is sighing more lately.

Uncle Reggie saunters into the front yard. Mom says he'll be staying with us through the holidays, until he "adjusts to being back."

"Can I keep you company?" he asks.

Max shakes his hair up and down. His palms are not sweating and his throat is not bobbing, which means that Max feels comfortable with Uncle Reggie — and I do, too. The three of us wait in the lawn's only warm spot, a small paradise in the late November sun.

"So what've you got going on at school today?" Uncle Reggie says, moving his dog tags under his shirt.

"Well," Max says, "I have a couple of quizzes, but after school my friend Charlie's helping me work on my rocket. We meet in the science lab. He . . . he doesn't talk a lot. Which is nice, sometimes."

"That's part of the reason I love dogs. They're much better listeners than they are talkers." Uncle Reggie plops down in the grass with me, even though it's damp. Dew soaks into his sweatpants. "I was thinking, maybe I could cook you all dinner tonight. What's your favorite?"

"Um . . . anything that's not tofu. Tofu made me really sick once, and then Cosmo ate some, and then he got sick . . . And it just wasn't good."

Uncle Reggie nods solemnly. "No tofu. Got it."

"Cosmo really likes cheese, though. Grilled cheese. Quesadillas. Anything with mozzarella."

"Should he be eating cheese?"

Max tilts his head back and forth. "Probably not."

This is true. With my gas, I can drive a whole group of humans from any room. Every once in a while, when I'm sleeping, I wake up to a clouded stench, and it's difficult to tell if it was me—or if another dog has crept in, farted, and run away. Max plugs his nose and says, "Cosmo, that's so gross," and then we laugh big laughs, even though I am not always to blame.

Uncle Reggie says, "I think I can still make this grilled cheese thing happen."

"Just . . ." Max says. "Just . . . don't leave any dishes on the counter. Mom and Dad fight about dishes a lot."

Uncle Reggie bites his lip. "I'll remember that."

We are silent for a moment before the yellow bus creaks to a stop by our mailbox. Max tucks his bag between his shoulders, runs up the steps, and waves back at us shyly with his beautiful hands.

"Learn stuff!" Uncle Reggie calls out.

I've given it a lot of thought over the years: where Max goes with his backpack full of things that taste so bland. School, I first assumed, must be like doggy day care. (Wide kennels. Plenty of rope toys. A communal area with grass and a small paddling pool.) I got most of the details wrong, but I do know that Max has friends at school. Two best friends, Charlie and Zoe—wonderful humans who always remember that my head is available for petting. Max can speak to them without losing his words. Every summer, the four of us catch baseballs and search for bullfrogs in the creek behind Zoe's house. We sit on her porch and eat pretzel sticks and listen to the birds make terrible noises in the trees.

I haven't seen Zoe lately. I'm worried that this might have something to do with me licking the top of her cat's head last August. That was an unfortunate incident. No one ever asked for my side of the story.

Uncle Reggie rubs my back in comforting circles and stares at the tail end of the bus. "He's a good kid, you know?"

Max? Yes! Max is the best kid. When I was younger and afraid of thunder, Max would wrap me in his favorite fuzzy blanket. "Cosmo burrito," he'd say, tucking my legs to my chest and pulling me close. We'd rock together until the clouds stopped banging like pots and pans. I never told him this, but sometimes I wished for thunder, just so he could burrito me.

Protect their hearts, Uncle Reggie had said.

And I must, because Max has always protected mine.

All day, I pace—claws tapping back and forth between rooms. I barely look at the TV, even though *Singin' in the Rain,* one of the greatest films ever made, is on Turner Classic Movies. When Uncle Reggie lets me out in the afternoon, the sun yellow in the sky, I refuse to leave the yard: I'm too focused on my thoughts, on how to avoid the separation with Max. In dog years, I'm the oldest of the Walkers: it's my responsibility, my *privilege,* to hold us together.

To brighten the mood, perhaps I should lick everyone's faces more often? Or bark less at the squirrels in our bushes? I could even shorten my poo time, choosing a spot at random without thorough inspection of the ground. But something tells me that I need to go bigger, bolder.

That night, we gather for a nice-smelling meal of grilled cheese and crunchy lettuce. I am very skillfully positioned by Max's chair, underneath the dining-room table. It feels like a cave, where my ancestors—the wolves—lived.

"Hope you're hungry," Uncle Reggie says.

"Thanks for doing this," Mom says.

"It's *great*," Max says. "You got the cheese right. Perfect stringiness."

Above me, they chew and chew. It takes them so long to eat. I've always marveled at how much easier it would be if they just ate with their faces pressed to their plates.

Emmaline takes a loud sip of her juice box. "Oooo! Oooo! Today Miss Janine read us a story about dogs and then we got to draw them in our journals and Cara said that my dog looked the most like a dog out of everyone's."

"Did you draw Cosmo?" Max asks, slyly feeding me a corner of his grilled cheese. I savor it, chewing slowly with my back teeth.

I hear Emmaline shake her head. "I drew Uncle Reggie's dog."

"I . . ." Uncle Reggie says. "I showed her a picture. Of Rosie. She's still in Afghanistan, but I'm hoping that we're going to see each other again real soon."

My ears tilt up. Sometimes when I listen—really *listen*—I discover extraordinary things. Like the fact

that trees are alive, and that sheepdogs are not dogs crossed with sheep, as I'd previously thought. Now I learn that Uncle Reggie trained German shepherds: dogs who run and jump like the wind is at their feet, who follow soldiers into combat zones and help keep us safe. He speaks of them as if they are people, too.

"I was thinking," he says, "you should bring Cosmo this Saturday."

I lift my head even more. Did I miss something? Bring me where?

Mom says, "Actually, that's a great idea. Max, you remember me telling you about the club, right?"

Max shifts in his chair. "Yeah. Okay. Cosmo would probably like that."

Might like *what*? I listen and listen, but they move on to other things. Mom and Dad head into the kitchen, where he says the dishwasher is too full.

She says, "Then take a few things out."

"Why didn't you run it? You've been home for *hours*," he says. "I don't know why this stuff doesn't get done."

They snap at each other like feral dogs, which I saw once behind the old movie theater in town. A male and a female with dark fur. When anyone tried to approach them, their lips curled. Their teeth gleamed like the sheepdog's on Halloween. I felt sorry for them. How badly were they hurting, to act like that?

As Mom and Dad begin to shout, ignoring everything else, Max offers me his hand to lick. His fingers wiggle. I recognize the gesture. It says: *Here I am. Notice me.*

If there's anything I've learned in my thirteen years, it's that everyone deserves to be seen.

Usually, I am exceptional on a leash. You cannot imagine the amount of restraint it takes to walk calmly and nobly by the side of your human when there are so many scents around you. But there is just something about this Saturday, about the breeze and the grass and the *energy*. In the parking lot of the local community center, Max and Uncle Reggie are joking back and forth, as people do, and I'm so overwhelmed by their joyousness that I tug. I lunge between cars. I chase my tail until I'm tangled up in my leash.

"What's gotten into you?" Max says, laughing. He bends down to lift my paws, releasing me from the entrapment.

Uncle Reggie winks. "Maybe he knows."

I like that he has such confidence in me.

Inside, the community center smells of those miniature cheese crackers that Max has in his lunch box.

Max looks around the lobby. "So, where is it?"

"I'm not entirely sure," Uncle Reggie says. "But the dogs will tell us."

I am just one dog, I think, although soon I understand what he means. I catch the scent of them. Beagles! Collies! Chihuahuas! Generally speaking, Chihuahuas are full of self-importance, and it is very difficult to win their friendship—but I'm still overjoyed to smell them in this human place. I've found that most buildings don't allow dogs, as if we are always sniffing for a spot to squat and relieve ourselves. (I only did that once, in a store with many garden hoses and aisles of dirt. I was just a puppy—it couldn't be helped—but the guilt has eaten at me for years.)

"This way," Max says, following the barks and howls. "Sounds like a party."

I tug more and more, sure that something good is just around the corner. When we enter a large room with fake grass, my excitement sparks, and I find myself shaking my head sharply, several times, to prove that this is real. Everywhere—there are dogs

everywhere, tails whipping back and forth, tongues wagging, noses to hindquarters. A dream? A beautiful dream?

Do you see them? I ask, glancing up at Max. *Do you see the dogs, too?*

"Whoa," he says, clearly taking it all in.

And Uncle Reggie says, "Whoa is right."

The sound of panting fills the air, along with a chorus of yips and howls. I'm having trouble focusing on one dog at a time. They're swirling together: gray coats and black coats, yellow coats and white coats. Half of me begs to join them—to lose myself in the swirl—but the other half is more cautious. I hesitate. I observe.

It isn't long before we hear a shriek, high above the noise. *"Noodles!"* A woman in a large sun hat begins chasing a corgi, who is bounding toward me with tiny leaps. Though I'm not usually a fan of small breeds, I do appreciate those with cheerful attitudes. And you can tell, by the way Noodles's tongue flits from her mouth, that her heart is pure. She crashes into my knee with a lopsided smile, and immediately starts poking my belly with her nose. On her breath is the scent of salmon—and now, of course, I am hungry.

"I'm *so* sorry," the woman says, the pockets of her

dress bulging with tennis balls. "You wouldn't think that she'd be fast, but she is *fast.*"

"Don't worry about it," Uncle Reggie says, waving his hand. "She seems sweet."

"She's a little nightmare is what she is." The woman grunts, trying to grab the leash—which is still attached to Noodles and twisting into knots. "Noodles, can you come back to Mommy?"

Noodles bows to me, stubby tail chopping the air. Her fur quivers: white, tan, and gleaming. Then she's barking, dashing, coiling the leash more.

"*Noodles!* Stop it!" the woman yells. "Goodness gracious, NOODLES!"

Max presses his hand to his mouth, and underneath it, I believe he is chuckling.

"Noodles?" he whispers after the woman leaves.

"If I ever get another dog," Uncle Reggie says, "I'll call her Pasta. Or Lasagna. Imagine calling that name across a park. 'Come here, Tortellini!'"

We have a good laugh over that one—but it hits me, just as a black Lab sweeps by, that I'm not completely sure why we're here. *The club,* Mom called it. I sift through everything I know about clubs, but these things, these things together, don't add up to a complete picture.

The black Lab barks. He's stopped several tail-lengths away, a young human at his side. Something about them is like me and Max; they appear as one. The boy kneels to tie his shoes, and I follow the laces with interest. I learned—a long time ago—that shoe-laces are not snakes, but you can never be too careful.

The boy catches me watching and grins. "Hey there," he says, scooting toward us, extending a hand for me to sniff. His ears are a bit pointy (terrier lineage, undoubtedly), and his hair is blond like mine. "Can I pet you?"

He leaves the decision up to me, which I appreciate. Some humans are incredibly rude, shoving their fingers into your face without so much as a warning. And yet people rarely do the same thing to one another: never have I witnessed Mom and Dad thrusting their hands into the fur of strangers. Yawning to show that I mean no harm, I bump the boy's fingers with my nose, and I'm astonished that he knows just where to scratch—right behind my ear, so good that my leg thumps.

"My dog loves this, too," the boy says, cocking his head at the Lab. "His name's Elvis, like the singer. My mom says he's 'much more than a hound dog,' which I think is a joke from a song. Anyway, he can be really strange. Like, whenever the water's running in the shower, he just sits on the bath mat, howling."

Elvis looks at us and burps. Several blades of grass dangle from the corners of his mouth, and I feel I must warn him about the dangers of eating too much greenery. He is much younger than I am—so many lessons to learn. His slender legs have a noticeable spring to them, and I can tell he wants to pounce on me in play. But he holds back, respectful like his human. I am old and he knows it.

Uncle Reggie nudges Max, gently telling him to say something. Respond. Use your words. And Max's nervousness fills the entire space. Uncle Reggie doesn't mean it. He doesn't understand how quickly Max's heartbeat travels through the leash.

The boy stands. "Cool shirt," he says to Max, who's wearing his favorite rocket T-shirt, the one that smells most like him. "I'm Oliver, by the way."

Max. He is Max. And I am Cosmo.

I would speak for both of us, if I could, if he wanted me to.

Before Max can work up the courage to say his name, a woman in the middle of the room claps her hands. She looks recently groomed, with gray hair that tumbles down her back like the fringe of a rope

toy, and long nails that—had they been mine—would clack against any hardwood floor.

"If everyone could just settle their dogs for a moment, please!" She waits, hands clasped in front of her. And it is so difficult, just so difficult to sit at a moment like this, with all the smells and the sounds.

"Sit," Max tells me. "Come on, Cosmo, *sit*. Please."

Elvis immediately plops down. Across the room, Noodles twirls in manic circles. And I half sit, then half sit again, before my butt touches the ground.

"Thank you!" the woman says. "Okay, great to see you all here today! I was a little worried that no one would show. Y'all have exceeded my wildest expectations. You must've heard about the prize!" She chuckles. "My name's Greta, and I started this club so we could come together, as a community, and practice the art of canine freestyle. I do mean 'art'! It's a sport, all right, but it takes *creativity* and *passion* and *drive*."

Greta lists these on her long, slim fingers, then pauses for a dramatic moment.

We stare, enraptured.

"I'll go ahead and tell you up front," she says, "canine freestyle isn't for everyone. It's fun—but it's tough. Really tough. As handlers, you'll have to train tirelessly with your dogs, practicing obedience, a variety of tricks, and heelwork to music. You and your dog must learn to move *together*. We'll be working toward the first annual Rainy-Day Dance Society's Canine Freestyle Championship, which is a statewide competition in August. There, a panel of judges will assess you on everything from timing and workmanship to personality and level of difficulty. I'm here to teach you, to guide you on your journey, and you're all here to support one another. Now, I know this is just a meet and greet, but I'd like to start us off with a demonstration — really kick this off in style! So, without further ado . . . Felix, place!"

The room stills. Out trots a border collie with a silver collar, practically glowing in the December light. And I stand there dramatically transfixed, pigeon toes pointed, as the border collie, his black-and-white coat sparkling, takes his place beside Greta. Then music starts, he bows — deeper and more elegantly than I thought possible — and begins to circle her, backward, to the beat of the song. *Backward!* Of all things!

"You think you could do that?" Uncle Reggie asks me.

But I can't even look at him, can't tear my eyes away.

Greta throws her arms to the side, and the col-

lie jumps through them, landing on his back legs, walking upright. And I know—I know deep in my bones—that I am witnessing something momentous, something holy. In all my life, I have never seen this kind of play.

Because they are not playing, I suddenly realize.

They are dancing.

Watch any classic film, and you will know: a dancer can command an entire room with a flick of his hips, a sharp wave of his arms. Nothing proves this more than *Grease.* Even during my first viewing, I recognized the power Danny and Sandy had over their audience as their hands flew.

And I recognized that I had the soul of a dancer.

Sometimes at night, after Max draws the blinds and the bedroom becomes dark, I imagine it: Max and me in *Grease,* dancing on the wooden floors of the basketball court, or perhaps on the school field. I imagine fresh-cut grass underneath my paws and the sun on our heads.

Back in the car, my mind spins so much that I'm forced to shove my nose into the crease of the seat. I close my eyes. All this time, thinking about *Grease,* thinking about those wonderful nights when my family twirled in the living room—all this time, and dogs can *dance.* Dancing isn't just in my soul! It's in my paws and my legs and the shake of my fur. And I have wasted so many years, believing I couldn't dance, believing I wasn't human enough.

Halfway home, a thought seizes me: Are all dogs *born* to dance? Please consider my reasoning.

1. Human dancing is very similar to dog play. We dip. We touch noses. According to the Discovery Channel, dogs have coexisted with humans for hundreds of thousands of years. Is it possible that early humans borrowed moves from dogs, such as dipping and twirling, and claimed them as their own?

2. The swish of a dancer's dress is like a dog's tail. Tell me that's a coincidence!

3. Monkeys are widely considered the most intelligent nonhuman animal. (In my opinion, this is just false. Any animal that flings its own poo could hardly be considered intelligent. But for the sake of argument, go with me.) Have you ever seen a monkey do the waltz? Or glide across the floor in elegant circles?

No. You wouldn't dream of it. But you *could* imagine a dog.

4. Classic dance films never feature dogs, although it is very clear to me now that dogs have an aptitude for dance. Did the Movie People discover, long ago, that dogs could outshine humans? Did they think the competition was too great, and so pushed dogs to the sidelines?

It's such a shame. *Grease* is spectacular now. Imagine how much more impressive it would be with a dog.

"Man, that was cool," Uncle Reggie says, pulling into our driveway and parking the car. "You really liked it?"

I know he's speaking to Max, not me, but I still lift my snout from the crease and bark twice, mighty and loud. *Yes! Yes!*

I will admit, though, that I was intimidated at the club. When I try something new (a trick, a command), I like to practice privately first. I like to envision myself succeeding, then take tentative steps in a quiet room. Perhaps this is a symptom of my age; failure is always a possibility—because of my bad hips, my stiff legs—so I hold back. And hold back. Until I can't hold back any longer.

Max unbuckles his seat belt and says, "Yeah, I

did." His voice has a strange, dreamy quality, and I wonder what's on his mind.

I can't even tell you what we had for dinner that night. (Probably nuggets—Dad says they're easy to prepare. They arrive in bags, packed suspiciously in frozen cubes, their scent locked beneath layers of cold. How can you trust something you can't smell?) Hours after the meal, Max and I seal ourselves into his room. The window is cracked open, curtains fluttering like pigeons, which would normally unsettle me to the core. But I'm too distracted by Max's laptop, by the picture he's showing me on-screen.

"I saw this online yesterday," he says. "This guy's a former astronaut, Leland Melvin. He served aboard the space shuttle *Atlantis,* and he snuck his two dogs into his NASA photoshoot: Jake and Scout. They're in his official portrait now. See, Cosmo?"

I do. In the photo, one dog licks the astronaut's ear, while the other assumes a pose I know well: half jump, half crouch, half in his human's lap.

"And I was thinking," Max continues, "that's what he's known for now. What he's *really* known for. Leland Melvin and his dogs—they've become this *thing,* together, and no one wants to see them apart. So what if . . ." He shifts on the bed, straightening his shoulders as I scoot closer onto his pillow. "This may sound kind of weird, but just hear me out, okay? After that woman at the dance club mentioned a prize, I looked it up. Next August, at the statewide canine freestyle competition, the winners get a walk-on role in a major dance movie. It'll be in all the theaters."

I blink, trying to process this as fast as I can.

Max's voice is a whisper now. "What if we win, Cosmo? You and me. What if we enter and *win*? Mom and Dad have been fighting more lately, and I just think . . . I just think that if we get in this movie, people would see us, and know us—*us,* together. And then it wouldn't even be a question. I wouldn't have to be like that kid at school who got separated from his dog. Mom and Dad would never break us up, after they see us, bigger than life. Maybe . . . maybe they'll even catch us practicing, and remember that dancing made us a family. That we should *stay* a family."

As his words disappear into the air, I find myself struggling to keep up. *Competition, movie, Mom and Dad*—the threads are all there, and yet . . .

"Here," he says, fiddling with his laptop. "Watch this."

We huddle closer together. Suddenly, a Jack Russell terrier flits across the screen as music tumbles around

us. The terrier hops on his back legs, like Emmaline does with a jump rope; he grapevines, leaps through his human's arms, ricochets off her hip. On the sidelines, judges watch them carefully, and a large audience claps in bursts.

"We could practice really hard at the club," Max is saying. "Learn everything we can. Dance like this."

And I'm listening. And I'm seeing.

The dog and his human—there's a connection. They are dancing as one.

It hits me all at once, like jumping off a dock into warm, warm water. I can see it so clearly: Max and me, on the set of a dance film. Max and me, shimmying across a field of green. Often, on TV, they show the same movies over and over, and I am constantly struck by their timelessness. These dancers! They will live, and live, and live—as long as someone is watching.

"What do you think?" Max asks, tucking his hand under my chin.

I think I am worried. I'll never move like the terrier on-screen, like the border collie at the club: my bones are too achy and my muscles are too stiff. Sometimes, on long walks with Max, my legs get weary and sore—and I hide it. I hide every wince, every urge to limp. Because I am walking him just as much as he is walking me, and he deserves that time outdoors. Could I do the same thing with dancing? Would I be good enough for him?

Max swings both feet out of bed, still waiting for my response. "Come with me," he says, and I follow—as I always do, as I always will.

It's unclear what we're looking for until we find him: Uncle Reggie, in the backyard. He's standing without a flashlight in the dark, the moon round and big, his neck craned to the sky.

"I'm trying to see what you see," Uncle Reggie says as we pad into the grass.

"That's Canis Major," Max says.

"Which one?"

"See that really bright star?"

"Yeah."

"That's Sirius, the nose. And now look down—see the triangle? That's the hindquarters. The whole thing's shaped like a dog."

"Well, I'll be," Uncle Reggie says as the three of us look up. "You're one smart kid, you know that?"

Max weaves his fingers together, his thumbs moving back and forth. "Can I ask you something?"

Uncle Reggie's brow furrows, concerned. "Of course, champ. Anything."

"Mom told me you're planning on working for the dance club?"

"Just volunteering. This is their first year, so they need the help. I was hoping to make some contacts before I start my own business."

"Training dogs?"

"Yep, training dogs."

Max pauses, the scent of his sweaty palms blooming in the night. "Can you train Cosmo and me, then? For the big freestyle dance competition? You said that you taught dogs to run into combat zones and sniff out bombs and stuff, so this should be easy, right? Cosmo listens when he has to. He does. And I'm a good listener, too. So please. *Please.* I . . . I want us to enter. And I'll do it anyway—but it would be so much easier if we had your help."

I'm finding it increasingly difficult to stay still. Everything about Max screams, *I want this*—and this startles me, the reality of the situation. Understanding the risk of separation is one thing, but I feel it now, really *feel* it. Max is pleading. He's pleading for us to stay together, which means we could be falling apart.

Uncle Reggie reaches down and laces his fingers through my fur. "I'd be happy to. But I guess, what makes you want to enter so badly?"

85

There's a long moment before Max answers. "I . . . I thought it could help with not being so shy and anxious all of the time."

My ears cock. Is he lying? Or half lying? Why doesn't he tell Uncle Reggie the whole truth?

"Dancing," Max says, "being up there in front of a crowd, it can only help, right? And Cosmo's not that old—he can move. I've seen him *really* move when he's motivated. I think we could win."

Uncle Reggie's jaw twitches beneath his skin. "Max, I don't want you to get your hopes too high . . . Some of these dogs, they're really well trained."

"Oh," Max says, head dipping just slightly. All the air gushes out of him. "You're probably right. Actually, forget I —"

"Wait. No forgetting," Uncle Reggie says, biting his lip. Something changes in him. He stands up taller. "You and Cosmo—well, you have a special bond. I can see it. I think we can make the dancing work, if you're partners. But I want this to be fun, okay?"

"So you'll train us?"

"I'll train you. We can even pick something from *Grease,* if you want. Your mom says you love those songs."

At this, I can no longer stay still. My whole

body quivers. And suddenly I understand some-thing—something else. Max isn't telling Uncle Reggie why we're competing. Because he is like me, afraid to name the sheepdog. We will never name our fears directly, or say them aloud; otherwise they will run out in front of us, wild like deer.

Max looks at me. "Well, Cosmo, are you up for it?"

It reminds me of the question Dad asked, all those years ago: Was I up for being a big brother? I give Max the same answer.

Yes.

A thousand times yes.

Counting is not one of my strong suits. Numbers—
anything higher than five—float easily from my mind.
But I concentrate on remembering *eight months and
eleven days,* as that's how long before the dance competition.

"It seems like a lot of time," Max says, tucking
himself in, right after Uncle Reggie agrees to train us.
"It'll probably fly by, though. What's good is we can go
to the dance club up to twice a week, and we'll practice
outside of class, too. We need that movie prize, Cosmo.
So we have to get this right."

I take his words to heart, and drink plenty of water
the next day. I sleep late, visualize success, and—that

night—stretch extensively at the edge of Max's bed. He pokes his head over his laptop, asking me, "What're you doing, silly dog?" I was hoping it would be obvious, although I'm not sure I've mastered this exercise. I can't check: there are no mirrors at my height. Even if there were, the dog in the mirror is not always me. Sometimes there is another golden retriever, copying my every move.

The following morning, as the first light peeks through Max's curtains, I feel ready. I wait as long as I can, sprawled on the bedroom rug, before succumbing to my urge: ignoring the creak in my spine, padding over to Max, and tickling him with my whiskers.

Slowly, he opens his eyes—and I pant a hello.

"Cosmo," he groans. "It's so early."

Yes! I tell him, licking his face, which tastes of salt and sleep and him. It's perplexing why Max never licks my face in return. Isn't this the obvious response? I can only assume that humans are like cats in this way; they cannot properly digest fur. My stomach can digest a wide variety of things. Napkins. Pizza crusts. Small amounts of cardboard. Humans miss out on so much joy: shoeboxes and paper envelopes, torn to shreds and eaten.

"Your breath smells like salami," Max says to me

now. We are nose to nose. I inch my head onto his pillow. "*Okay,* you're right. I should get up."

Still in his astronaut pajamas, with the little spacemen on the sides, he slips into his sneakers and trails into the kitchen, where Uncle Reggie is making coffee that smells tremendously strong. I am not allowed coffee, even though older humans seem to swear by it. *I am old, too,* I always tell them, trying not to feel left out.

"Morning," Uncle Reggie says. "I thought you were sleeping in."

Max tilts his head toward me. "Cosmo wants a walk."

"I can take him out, if you want to go back to bed?"

"Thanks, but it's not so bad." Peering around the house, his gaze travels down the hall toward Mom and Dad's room. Their door is closed, no noises underneath it. "Actually, I think I like the quiet."

"Quiet's good," Uncle Reggie says, drinking his coffee so smoothly. His lips press together in a way that mine do not, his tongue firmly in his mouth. If you really think about it, it's a remarkable thing. "Well, if both of you are up, we should take advantage of it. How about some training?"

"That's what I was hoping," Max says.

I let them believe this was their idea.

In the empty cul-de-sac, Max rubs the sleep from his eyes, and I lift my nose to sniff the world. It's funny: our neighborhood used to feel infinite. I used to think the streets and the sidewalks went on forever. The older I get, the smaller they become. *Cookies.* The thought takes hold of me. There are cookies in the pocket of Max's pajamas. The lovely outline of them pokes through the fabric. Chicken? Are they chicken flavored?

"Cosmo's food motivated," Uncle Reggie says, as if he can read my thoughts. "So we'll use that. Every time he gets something right, give him a treat. It'll reinforce the behavior."

This reminds me—quite suddenly—of the cookie trick. Last year, instead of merely sitting for a treat, Max taught me to balance one on my nose. And let me tell you, it is not easy: the balance or the patience, as the scent is so close to your nostrils. In moments of weakness, I snapped the cookies from my snout in clean swoops, devouring them and burping with gusto.

But as I think about it, that seems so simplistic compared to dancing. The kibble from last night churns in my belly, and with it comes a sense of fear—of help-lessness. Who am I, to do this?

"Now," Uncle Reggie says, "I know that Cosmo has arthritis, but movement is really good for that. The more he moves, the better he'll be; I'm just saying that so you don't worry. I've also been watching some canine freestyle competitions on YouTube, to see what the current standards are. And the best routines give you a *feeling*." He scrunches up his hands, like he's trying to squeeze the air. "I know we don't have a song yet, but I want you to think about what emotion you're trying to convey. Cosmo will pick up on that."

I curl my back legs underneath me, lying down as Max answers, "I like the idea of *Grease*—a happy song."

"Good," Uncle Reggie says. "Now give me a happy memory."

"Right now?" Max asks, swallowing.

"Mmm-hmm, right now."

"Okay . . . um . . . let me think." My jaw rests on the tip of his shoe, and his toes flex beneath it. "It's not a big thing—but one time, Cosmo chased an entire herd of deer in Sawyer Park. It was like a flip switched in his brain, and he wouldn't come back to us no matter how loud we called, so all of us were running after him—running and running—until finally he stopped and looked back. He seemed really surprised to see us.

And Mom just started laughing, then we all did."

Uncle Reggie beams, backing up. "Great—now I want you to think about that memory as you and Cosmo are walking toward me. Just walking, that's it. We're going to start really simple."

I can do that, I think, hoisting myself to a stand. My legs tremble slightly, as they often do after I've been lying on my side. But I keep that moment in mind, when the soft ground was beneath my feet, when I was running after the white tails of deer. Max was right: a feeling overtook me. There was no sound and no sky; I was one with the earth. What I remember most is turning around, as my tongue lolled and my pace slowed—and they were *there.* My family. All my life, I'd followed them. It never occurred to me that they'd follow me, too.

"Cosmo," Max says now, "with me."

With me is a command I love: staying by his side, placing one paw in front of the other. We walk joyously. We walk as if we are filled with light.

"Eyes up," Uncle Reggie says, still traveling backward. "Stand tall." When we've journeyed down the street, from mailbox to mailbox, he stops and hands me a treat. "Great. Really good. Let's keep that energy for every step we learn."

Max pats my head, and a sudden confidence fills me. I can't explain it. It's like a starburst, a brilliant piece of sky. And I decide to seize that feeling. All those years, as I witnessed my family spinning elegant circles on dance nights, I made assumptions: I will never stand on my back legs for long or twirl like a human with finesse and grace. But as a soft wind floats through the neighborhood—right here, right now—I spin smoothly to the best of my ability, putting all of me into all of it.

My neck aches; the arthritis in my legs is a dull burn.

But the world, it opens.

Dancing! I am *dancing*!

Max feeds me a cookie from his pocket. "Good job, Cosmo," he says, and then to Uncle Reggie: "I didn't even need to tell him what to do! He just did that!"

I know we are all thinking the same thing: a giraffe could never master a trick so easily. Movie stardom, here we come.

"That's . . . that's actually really great," Uncle Reggie says. "Now let's see if we can get him to do it on command, maybe with a hand movement."

We repeat the exercise over and over—*Cosmo, spin!*—as Max twirls his finger. Sunlight spreads across the neighborhood. In the background, humans open their blinds and shuffle onto their porches, morning coffees in hand. When they wave at Max, Uncle Reggie, and me, I see it on their faces: the astonishment, the pride. *We have a dancing dog among us.*

"I think that's really good for today," Uncle Reggie says.

Max's eyebrows pinch together. "But we've barely started."

"We've been doing this for half an hour—and we don't want to overwhelm him on day one. Don't worry. There's plenty of time."

I hope that Uncle Reggie is right.

When Max goes to school the following week, I practice on my own. Occasionally a classic dance film
flickers across the TV, and I study the moves with
renewed interest, testing—in the privacy of the
study—how it feels to hop, bounce, prance. You might
call me a creature of habit; the faster we incorporate
dancing into our daily routine, the greater our chances
of winning the walk-on movie role.

"What's with Cosmo?" Mom keeps asking. "He
never used to bark like this."

But she doesn't scold me. Neither does Dad. I think
they know, deep down, that I'm barking for us.

Soon it's the coldest day of the year so far, and Mom suggests—as Max and Uncle Reggie are bundling up before we head to the dog club—that I might need a sweater. Such a thing exists, hidden in the bowels of the closet; I know because I stuffed it there. Dark blue. Woolly. Hideous. Every time I wore it, two thousand years of evolution laughed in my face. Thankfully, Max guides me out the door before Mom starts looking, and then we're whizzing down sleepy roads, all the way to the community center.

As we pad onto the club's fake grass, with its smell of plastic bags that crinkle in the rain, I immediately spring into action. *Give me a command,* I tell Max, gazing up. *And I will follow.*

"I think someone's waving at you," Uncle Reggie says at the same time. Clusters of humans and dogs are wandering around, so it's difficult to spot him right away. But oh! Oliver! The boy from the last class is signaling Max eagerly, fingers waggling.

Uncle Reggie nods. "Go say hello."

Max begins to say, "Maybe I'll just hang out over—"

But I'm already pulling strongly at the leash, weaving through a pod of beagles.

I've noticed that some humans have trouble making friends. For dogs, it's easy. You smell one another, drink respectfully from the same water dish, and rejoice in everlasting friendship. If you're a person, there is just so much to remember: shake here, show your teeth there, nod your head but not too hard. I play my part where I can.

Stopping in front of Oliver's dog, Elvis, I bow. He bows. We touch noses, sniff beneath tails, gently bite each other's necks. His black fur looks sleek as he dashes around.

"Sorry if his breath is kind of bad," Oliver says to Max and me. "He drank toilet water this morning."

Max scrunches up his whole face. "Gross."

"I guess there are worse things he could've gotten into. I mean, he *has* gotten into worse things. But this morning he just snuck up on me when I was brushing my teeth. *Wham!* He head-butted the door open and rushed in, and I was trying to pull him back by his collar, and toilet water was flying everywhere. Well, not *everywhere*. But—you know—into his mouth. And on the floor. I gave him some biscuits afterward and they're real strong-smelling, because I thought that would cover it up. But now that I think about it, toilet water doesn't actually smell that bad—so maybe it's just the biscuits."

"Maybe," Max says, his voice hesitant. He strokes the smooth underside of Elvis's chin.

"Anyway, I hope he learns something today. We haven't tried any tricks yet. Elvis doesn't know that many tricks in general, unless you count the howling thing or barking at dogs on TV. I doubt he'll be a good dancer, but that doesn't really matter—because it's fun just hanging out with him. Hey, am I talking too much?"

Max blinks, his cheeks heating. "What?"

"Talking," Oliver repeats. "Too much. My gran says I do that sometimes. The talking thing. You'd probably know that already, except we go to different schools. I go to Parker Middle and you must go to Ridgeway, right? Ridgeway seems nice. I hear they have a cool science lab."

Max smiles.

In the center of the room, Greta—the dance club instructor—clears her throat very loudly, like she's swallowed a bee. I can relate to this, as bees are immensely tempting. Catching them is an accomplishment.

"Welcome back!" Greta says. "I hope that everyone had a nice time at the meet and greet! Now it's time to get down to business. For the next eight months, we'll be focusing on a different move every class, and then start putting them all together. Things like bowing, backing up, weaving through legs, spinning, rolling, moving sideways. As you'll recall, this is part of a *statewide competition*! With a grand prize! And I'd *love* to see a dog from our little club win."

Max peers down at me, and I know he's thinking: *Us. This needs to be us.* Mom and Dad have to see us on the big screen—flawless, unstoppable, together. Otherwise the risk is too great: me and Max, in separate houses, apart.

"So," Greta says, "remember that you can use treats during practice, when the dogs are learning, but on competition day, no. That's an automatic disqualification. Make your hand cues as subtle as possible. Today we'll be marching in place. Have your treats ready! I'll show you the command with my dog first, give a short demonstration, and then each of you will get a chance to try it. Sound good? Now, if everyone can make a big circle and move their dogs two steps to the—"

Noodles darts.

"Goodness gracious!" her human yells. "Noodles! *Noodles!*"

Never in my life have I seen a corgi run with such recklessness, such passion. Her pink collar glitters as she streaks through the room; her leash whips behind her. So fast. It is all so fast: the eruption of chaos. Elvis begins to howl, and I can see the temptation in

his eyes. Should he join the chase? He takes one last look at Oliver before dissolving into a black streak, his strides long and quick. Two Chihuahuas follow, gnashing with their tiny teeth. Behind them are a bulldog, a husky, and a cocker spaniel.

And that is when I spy it.

In the midst of the chaos—or perhaps *causing* the chaos—is the sheepdog. Demon! Devil! I'm so shocked that my throat dries. It struts in, deliberately slow. Oh, I can smell it! I can smell it from across the room! A musky scent, like old bologna, mixed with something mysterious and strange. As it shakes out its enormous puffball of fur, my mind flashes back to Halloween: the sheepdog in that menacing tutu and fairy wings, prancing around the yard as if it owned the world. At any moment, I expect its eyes to glow red.

But it is so cruelly casual, so coy. A pink bow tie pops above its collar, and it sits like a good dog, the leash limp in its human's hand. On the other end of the leash is a middle-aged woman with sheepdog ancestry, her clothes baggy, her hair puffed. She shuffles in at the same pace, taking her time. Slippers flap on her feet.

"Newcomers!" Greta shouts above the *woof*s. "Welcome!"

Welcome? I know that human noses are remarkably inferior, but surely Greta can *see* what's happening. Look at how it lounges as chaos swirls around it! My hackles rise to their fullest, my legs trembling with rage. Because I know. I *know.* The sheepdog is here to win the competition. To steal the glory, the movie role.

To separate Max and me once again.

As a rule, I don't growl. I'm a golden retriever—a family dog. I have a reputation to uphold. Yet, as the sheepdog's eerie glance falls in my direction, something deep within me rumbles awake. A primal sensation. A wolf-like urge. From the pit of my belly comes a loud snarl—and sure, to the outsider, it sounds like a *woof.* But the sheepdog knows. The sheepdog hears.

I will not, I say. *I will not let you destroy us.*

The sheepdog is unpredictable. Sometimes, it dances with the grace of a horse. Other times, its movements are rough, shuddering, and I am unsure whether to lunge forward or back slowly away. In the middle of the room, Greta is demonstrating with her border collie how to march in place—front paws lifting, right then left—and I'm listening as well as I can. But one eye is on the sheepdog, always on the sheepdog. Who knows what destruction it might unleash if I let it wander from my sight?

"He needs to raise his paws a little higher," Uncle Reggie says.

Max reaches down and delicately lifts my foreleg—up, up. "That's it, Cosmo. Good boy. You want a treat?"

I take the chicken snack with the side of my mouth (if I turn my head completely, the demon dog could slip from view), and I do not enjoy the flavor as much as I'd like, although it is salty and good. Across the way, my dance rival has mastered the march with startling precision—its paws higher than mine, its movement crisper—and a sinking feeling is beginning to register: the sheepdog is a better dancer.

"Maybe we can try to link those moves together," Uncle Reggie is saying. "The march and the spin."

But I'm thinking about the sheepdog's fur. Is its fluff a natural advantage? Every swish is exaggerated. It doesn't even have to try!

Max nods. "Okay. Let's do it."

As they guide me through the *spin, march, spin,* I vow to practice twice as hard as the sheepdog, because in dance films, that is what the hero does. He proves his worth. He proves his heart. Often there is a theme song, playing inspirationally in the background as the hero trains, and he must perform other tasks to help his journey: climbing stairs, or punching bags filled with heavy things, or doing push-ups on solid ground. As a dog, my options are more limited, and stairs are definitely out of the question—not with my hips. But I will do what I can, *all* I can. At the forefront of my mind, I hold the images of Max and me on a movie set, of Mom and Dad watching us on the big screen, understanding just how much we belong together.

Though the rest of class is a frenzied blur, I manage to link the moves, the first steps in our routine. Elvis conquers the march, too; as we leave the club, I catch him in the corner of my eye, carefully strutting across the room. He's second-guessing himself—it's obvious by his hesitation, every few steps—yet he's a natural dancer. Noodles is the opposite. Even a giraffe could see that she lacks basic obedience skills! Although there *is* something special about her boldness, something the judges might like.

"You did really well today," Max tells me that night. "Hey, did you hear Greta say that the casting director is coming to the competition? He'll be scoring us along with the judges. We really just need to keep up the hard work."

So, in the days before Christmas, we practice every morning. We push ourselves. Uncle Reggie drinks his coffee, Max carries the cookies, and I gain ground: step by step, trick by trick, with determination. Soon, I can jiggle my hindquarters on command! I can rock my head back and forth to a beat. And it strikes me that *I* am not being trained—not just me. Max and I are training each other.

Spin! I say.

And he spins.

"Shake!" he says.

And I shake.

Uncle Reggie is surprised by how quickly I'm catching on, but I know Max understands what's at stake if I fail. He knows about sniffing his ears at night and watching rocket launches on his laptop; about trips to the burger store, when strangers pass bags of food through our car windows, and he'll feed me small bites of meat with open palms. Emmaline will be six and then seven, Max thirteen and then fourteen—and I might miss it. If we're separated, I might miss all of it.

"I've been looking at some more YouTube competitions," Max says one morning. "And lots of dogs do this paw-hop thing. Can we try that move?"

Uncle Reggie says, "Go for it."

We begin with "paw" and work our way toward the hop. Max demonstrates, his feet kicking off the ground, as Uncle Reggie lifts a treat to the sky. Naturally, I follow it, reaching and reaching and *reaching*. Both of my front paws lift off the ground. It's just a second.

But it is a glorious second.

In dancing, repetition is key. It doesn't matter if you perform the trick correctly the first time. What matters is *constantly* getting it right, so that when competition day arrives, you are ready. You don't even have to think: your body already knows. Thus, we repeat the paw-hop many times, and afterward the three of us relax on the lawn, watching the sun spread farther and farther into the sky. The pavement is so cool that time of day, and I like to rest my body on the grass, my head on the sidewalk.

"I've got to admit," Uncle Reggie says, propped up on his elbows, "Cosmo's impressing me."

"Yeah?" Max says.

"Yeah. But don't be surprised if he hits a wall soon. He's learned about five new things in the last week. It might start to get jumbled."

"Oh," Max says, biting his lip. "Okay."

We wait. We wait for the light to wash over everything. And somewhere in the neighborhood, the sheepdog howls.

The more we dance, the more I sense a shift in my
family, even just slightly. Now, most of the time, the
smell in the kitchen is roast beef, and Uncle Reggie's
laughter bounces down the hall early in the morning.
I love how his blankets are folded neatly on our couch.
The turkey bacon is no longer there, under the third
cushion, but I am glad that he found it—that I was
able to share something so special with him.

In the mornings, Max and I work on things like
sliding, rolling, and maintaining hand-to-eye contact
during the dance. "Right here," he says, drawing an
invisible line between us. "Look here."

The performance and the movie prize are always on our minds.

We relax some evenings, though. Max has even started reading to me before bed. Sore from exercise, I rest my legs on his comfy blanket.

We eat our mac 'n' cheese for dinner and tuck ourselves into bed at night. The good noises return: water rushing and curtains opening, Emmaline giggling at those cartoon rabbits on TV. We even get my picture taken with Santa. Everyone tosses "good boy, Cosmo" in my direction; I try to look thoughtful and distinguished as the camera flashes, although Max tells me that my lip was caught on my upper canine tooth the whole time. "Silly dog," he says, and we all laugh as we wrap presents, decorate the tree, and watch *The Muppet Christmas Carol* on the big TV in the living room.

No one cries, that I can hear. No one has to.

Which is why I'm horrified when the cardboard box arrives.

"Did you order something?" Dad asks, slicing the tape.

The back of my neck pricks, fur rising. I'm not sure how I know, but I can feel it: an evil presence has invaded our home.

"Not that I recall," Mom says, digging through the plastic and pulling out a piece of paper. "That explains it. Max and Emmaline, come in here! Grandma sent you a gift."

They skip in from their bedrooms, dressed in day clothes, and tear through the packaging. I let loose a series of *woof*s — a warning cry — but Dad shushes me, a finger to his lips. Why can't they sense it, the change in the air? I wait anxiously by the edge of the table, my tail tucked, trying to get a glimpse into the box.

Emmaline discovers it first, raising the little demon to the light.

A sheepdog. It's a miniature sheepdog, with puffy fur and eyes that glint with madness.

"What is it?" Max asks.

What *is* it? The culmination of evil! The villain of the neighborhood! My archenemy!

"It's probably supposed to go on the Christmas tree," Dad says, instructing Max to place it low on the branches. *Too low,* I think. It can jump safely off — maybe even crawl to our back door, maybe even let the big sheepdog in.

That night, I give the demon a wide berth, but I study it. Noting its position, which never moves.

Noting its smile, sinister and toothy. Max says that the dog wears little red slippers on its paws. *A color for Christmas?* I wonder. *Or a color for blood?*

The next day, Mom and Dad begin to fight again, and the worry bites at me with full force: Max and me, in different houses, separated. There are hours when it feels like the whole house is shaking. Uncle Reggie ushers Max, Emmaline, and me into the backyard, where we pretend not to hear and pretend not to see. Later, I find Max curled up in the bathtub, without the water running. I whine and rest my jaw on the edge of the tub, but he doesn't look at me. He's too busy staring at Emmaline's plastic duck, balanced on his knees. As I've said, ducks are very boring. I know that other things are on his mind.

"Do you really think this will work?" Max finally asks me, setting the duck aside. "The movie thing? Us, dancing?"

Yes, I say, because it has to. Settling onto the bath mat, my chin on the soft fabric, I decide that something must be done about the miniature sheepdog. When we let it inside out house, we let sadness in with it.

In most cases, I immediately face my enemies and my fears. The laundry room used to terrify me, for example, but its rattling and eating of clothes no longer sends a chill up my spine; I stood by the door for three wash cycles in a row, immersing myself in its sounds. Similarly, sticking my head out of a moving-car window held little appeal—until I tried it. And *wow*! Let me tell you, there is just something about the wind whistling past your ears, a breeze on your face. I learned to love the way my eyelids fluttered as we sped along an empty stretch of highway.

But the sheepdog has always felt different. It's a great unknown, a dark spot in my vision. And I don't want to underestimate my miniature opponent.

I want to be ready.

The next two days, the house is very, very quiet after Mom and Dad leave for work and Uncle Reggie takes Emmaline and Max outdoors. I'm not sure where they go. All I know is that, occasionally, the doorbell rings; I enjoy this, because it breaks up my day, and I can bark at the man who delivers our mail. We receive lots of packages, some wrapped in cardboard, some wrapped in colorful paper. I sniff them all, thoroughly, to see if another sheepdog awaits us.

On Christmas Eve, Emmaline bursts into Max's room wearing a glittery gold halo. She hops. She bounces. "Mommy says it's time to go." Then she launches herself onto Max's bed and buries her face

in my fur, her warm fingers on my back. "I wish you could come, Cosmo."

So do I.

Emmaline is an angel in our town's nativity play, where she is supposed to sit with a flock of animals. I cannot remember if any of them are sheepdogs—and the image won't leave me, of Emmaline in a manger, long strands of gray-and-white fur curling all around her.

"I'm ready," Max says, shutting his laptop and ruffling the top of my head. "Guard the house, okay?"

A tall order. I'm not sure he understands just how tall it is.

Soon, the five of them are gone. I hear the garage door closing, the minivan pulling away from the mailbox. And I know it's time. For the safety of my family, I must face the miniature sheepdog alone.

When I round the corner into the living room, its sinister expression is the first thing to greet me. I stop short on the rug, gathering courage. Then I snarl with my canine teeth, rushing forward, clamping my jaws around the demon dog, and shaking it violently.

Oh, sweet victory! How good it feels!

Although, soon afterward I realize I've made a mistake. The material is so thick, so wiry, that it hurts to chew. Swallowing is the only option. I tilt my head back, hoping for the best. But the little demon hangs on, its slippered paws clinging to the inside of my throat.

To my credit, I refuse to panic—not immediately. This is easily the fourth time that an object has become stuck in my throat. The first two were in my youth: sticks at the park, gobbled too soon. The third was the remnants of a rope toy covered in goose poop. (If you have ever truly smelled goose poop, you would understand the irresistibility.) But I do recognize that this time is different, as no one is around to rescue me.

I paw at my snout, trying to loosen the sheepdog. I hack and wheeze.

I begin to worry.

And then I begin to panic, my heart thumping like paws on pavement. *This cannot be the way,* I think. I cannot go out this way. Our movie role! Max and I have barely gotten to dance.

There's a lightness in my head, a brief flash of sky—

The front door opens.

Max's footsteps, Max's voice: "Uncle Reggie forgot his wallet! You seen it, Cosmo? Are you —?" He pauses in the foyer, taking in the scene. I retch. Brilliant as

Max is, he understands right away, and I'm reminded in a great burst just how fiercely I love him.

"Oh, oh, no," he says, alarm rushing across face. "DAAAD! MOOOM!"

Everything happens quickly after that: Max prying open my mouth with shaky hands; Mom, Dad, and Uncle Reggie rushing across the lawn; Dad shoving his fingers into the back of my throat and removing the blockage.

"You ate the sheepdog?" Mom asks me moments later, staring at the slobbery mess in Dad's palm. "Why on earth would you do that?"

I'm so blinded by relief (I can breathe again!) that I don't answer. What I would've said was *Because someone needed to.*

"We can't leave him now," Max says to Mom. "Can't he . . . Is there any way that Cosmo can come with us?"

Dad says, "There's going to be nowhere for him to—"

"Please," Max said. "*Please.* I really need to have Cosmo there. I . . . What happens if . . . I can't lose him."

Uncle Reggie blows air from his cheeks. "I'm sure we can figure out something." He looks at Mom and Dad. "Come on, it's Christmas Eve."

So I'm loaded carefully into the back seat of the minivan, Max and Emmaline on either side, the radio bursting with an upbeat song called "Frosty the Snowman." If you are unfamiliar with the song, it's about a snowman who finds a magical hat. He comes alive. And the first thing Frosty does? He dances.

There's something inspiring in that.

Max has to sneak me into the theater. "Quiet," he says. "Be as quiet as you can." And I am, my paws barely making a sound. I slump between two seats, and a few people wish me merry Christmas, petting my head with kind strokes.

Emmaline is wonderful in the play, although it startles me that she has wings like a bird: monstrous things with feathers that float to the floor. (I do not bark at her, or even whimper, when she waves at me from the stage.) Afterward we celebrate with apple pie and hot cider in the church basement, and I'm allowed a few laps from a paper cup, Max's hands steady at my height. Back home, he feeds me carrot sticks under the glow of the twinkle lights. "Don't tell anyone," he says, massaging the folds of my neck. "They're supposed to be for the reindeer."

I chomp softly.

I know how to keep a secret.

Soon, Emmaline goes to bed in her special footie pajamas. "The ones with the snowmen," she tells me proudly, wiggling her toes. Mom and Dad head to their room, where paper rustles. I can hear friendly noises: tugging at ribbons, cutting tape. In the living room it is only Uncle Reggie, Max, and me. We plop on the floor, watching the sheepdog-less tree glimmer and blink.

"You know," Max says, "a couple years ago, Cosmo knocked down the Christmas tree."

Uncle Reggie laughs. "Really?"

"We came back from the grocery store and he looked so guilty. There were ornaments everywhere."

I remember this well. I could run, back then — and I was chasing the flicker of the lights, round and round, when I lost grip on the hardwood floor and tumbled stomach-first into the base of the tree. There was a great *whomp* as it fell, engulfing me in its branches. Later Max told me a human saying: *If a tree falls in a forest and no one is around to hear it, does it make a*

sound? As I thought about this, I decided the question was flawed: trees never really exist alone. There is always an animal, like me, to hear them fall.

"You're really lucky to have a dog like Cosmo," Uncle Reggie says. "But I'm sure you know that."

Max nods. "He's the best dog in the world."

I sit a little higher.

"And you know you can talk to him," Uncle Reggie says. "You can talk to me, too. About whatever you want. I think we're both good listeners."

Max shifts, his hands blue under the twinkle lights. "Well, there is something."

"Name it."

"You don't have to answer."

"I will."

"What's going to happen . . . ?" Max begins, twisting his lips, like he doesn't know how to finish. "What's going to happen with your dog, Rosie? Do you miss her?"

Uncle Reggie runs a hand over his head, which is softer now with new fur. I wonder if he has curls like Max, if one day Max will wear his hair in long braided strands. "I miss her all the time. Every day. She's my best friend—but she's got a job, and our jobs aren't the same anymore."

119

"You'll be able to get her back though, right?"

"I'm trying," Uncle Reggie says. "And sometimes that's all we can do."

Max looks down at his knees. "Do you think she'd be a good dancer?"

"Rosie is a good *everything*. She's super smart. Maybe a little too smart. Back at the base, we called her 'Houdini Dog,' because she could get out of anything. Leashes. Harnesses. Kennels. Once, I even left her in my room, and she turned the doorknob with her teeth. Oh, and she *loves* peanut butter."

Max smiles. "Cosmo does, too."

"I think that's a dog thing."

A few noises in the house: faucets running water, a tree branch tapping on the window.

"Did your mom ever tell you," Uncle Reggie says, "that in the military, the dogs pick the trainer? All us humans line up in a field, and the dogs sniff their way over to us—choose who they want. And they rank above us, too."

Max raises his eyebrows. "Really?"

"Yep, so if they disobey a command, they don't get in trouble. Rosie's usually a good listener, but there are some times—man!" He laughs. It gets caught in his throat. "*Man,* I love that dog."

I drift in and out as they sit in comfortable silence, and as we trail to bed, I wonder how Rosie can stand it, the separation. All those miles and miles in between. So I lie awake, listening to Max breathing; I watch his belly rise, and think about how the Movie People will capture his best angles—because all his angles are best.

In the morning, we wake to nice smells in the kitchen. Cinnamon rolls! Eggs! Milk! Max rubs his eyes, then whips off the covers, reaching down to pat the crest of my head. "I really think you're going to like what I got you," he says. I tell him, *I hope it is toilet paper. Or, at the very least, a cat.*

Outside the door, Emmaline greets me, waving something fluffy in her hands. I suddenly realize what it is: a pair of reindeer antlers. They go immediately on top of my head, pressing into the grooves behind my ears. How embarrassing. This is worse than the turtle costume. Maybe this is my price for eating the carrot sticks.

"That. Is. Adorable," Mom says, grinning.

"He doesn't like it," Max says, voicing my opinion.

Uncle Reggie just laughs, and Dad pulls down the long socks from the mantle. Emmaline unwraps a new superhero cape while Max unboxes a set of moon rocks. He holds them breathlessly. I wish I had been the one to give them to him.

"Wait," Max says suddenly. "I want Cosmo to open his gift."

"You open it for him," Mom says, dragging away the ribbons. "After last night, I don't really trust him with anything in his mouth."

So Max picks at the paper and unwraps the present. "You like it?" he asks, wagging a stuffed pig in front of my nose. Its stomach *oink*s.

"Call him Mr. Oinkers," Emmaline declares. "Cosmo and Mr. Oinkers."

While I don't dislike the name, it does seem a bit obvious. Like calling Dad "Mr. Human." Cautiously, I grab the toy with my mouth and start to appreciate the feel of it, the plushness. All the stuffed toys in my life have led to disappointment: I work so hard to soak them with my scent, and then, as suddenly as they enter my life, they are tossed in the wash. In the *wash*! I'm hopeful that Mr. Oinkers will meet a different fate.

After the paper is put away, I manage to paw off my antlers, and my family wraps themselves in scarves. We head outside for a walk, the frost disappearing from the grass. Emmaline jumps over the

cracks in the sidewalk. I try to join her, leaping and bounding the best that I can. Despite all the ways my body aches, this is my thirteenth Christmas—and I want to enjoy it.

When Grandma and Grandpa arrive around noon, I'm surprised. Were they always coming? But I take it in stride. If Max and Emmaline are happy to see them, then I should be, too.

"I brought pound cake all the way from home!" is the first thing Grandma says, though I cannot figure out why anyone would want cake from the pound. From what I've seen on TV, it seems like a terrible place for baking. She is still wearing one of her enormous sheepdog sweaters. The fur of it shivers. Behind her, Grandpa rushes in with a bundle of flowers, which Dad says smell fantastic, although it's clear to me that no animal has urinated on them. I sniff and sniff. They could smell so much better.

Grandpa unloads the suitcases, helps Dad blow up a mattress in the living room, and heads toward the backyard, where I'm sitting with my favorite tennis ball, the scruffy one, with the chew marks. All of a sudden, he bends down, grabs the ball, and waggles it very close to my face. "You want it? Go get it!" I see his arm dart through the frigid air, but the ball never leaves his hand. I cock my head to the side, realizing: *A trick! It's a trick!*

"Go get it," he keeps saying, trying to hide the toy behind his back. "Go on!"

I am not so easily fooled.

Eventually, he does toss the ball—near the squirrel bushes—and I fetch it with annoyance, dropping the ball by his toes. A thought seizes me. I am going to trick him right back. As soon as Grandpa swoops down to retrieve the ball, I grab it *first*! And it feels good to trot away, tail swishing victoriously, ball firmly between my teeth.

I keep waiting for things to sour, for Grandma and Grandpa to taint the happiness. But as we gather around the table that night—me, slightly underneath the table—I start to believe that today will be all right. We laugh. Uncle Reggie sings "Jolly Old Saint Nicholas." We eat so much ham that our bellies are round. And right before bed, Max feeds me an oatmeal cookie. It is so magnificently tasty that I drool all over his leg.

"You really are a good dog," he says to me as he's drifting off to sleep.

And it is a good day, I think, cuddling Mr. Oinkers. A very good day.

16

Sometimes, when I can't sleep, I try to remember my happiest moments. They come to me in bright flashes: A summer beach trip with Max. Emmaline's third birthday party. That one movie night when an entire bowl of popcorn tipped to the floor, and I scooped every kernel into my mouth.

The morning after Christmas, while Max sleeps in, I take the opportunity to go over the dance steps in my mind: *spin, march, paw-hop.* We have part of a choreographed routine—and if we're going to win that walk-on movie role, I need to memorize it perfectly. I've placed Mr. Oinkers on his side and shoved my snout beneath him, so that his body is covering my eyes. It helps block out the rest of the world. It helps me focus.

"You can bring him with you, if you'd like," Max says on our way to the dance club that afternoon. He squeezes the toy's plush tummy, tempting me, but I politely decline. The sheepdog would undoubtedly see my pig and want to claim him as its own, soiling the fibers of Mr. Oinkers's fur with its sheepdog drool. I am fighting so many battles already; I'm not sure I can handle even one more.

Uncle Reggie brings leftover cookies to the dance club that day: small glittery biscuits with sugar that crumbles. Oliver stuffs several in his mouth at once, then tosses a piece to Elvis, who catches it impressively with his front teeth.

"Get anything good for Christmas?" Oliver asks, cheeks full.

Max fiddles with my leash. "Yeah. Um, some moon rocks, and . . . uh . . . the new *Star Wars* comics."

"Dude!" Oliver bursts. "When can I come over? Don't tell me any spoilers . . . Oh. I didn't mean to just invite myself to your house. Sorry. But seriously, can I come over?"

Max nods, and the nervousness evaporates from his skin.

As the humans indulge in a multitude of leftover cookies, all of us dogs crowd around the water dish in good cheer. For a few moments, I almost think I'm lucky: that by vanquishing the miniature sheepdog, I've beaten the big sheepdog as well. It isn't here! It isn't prancing ominously in the corner, shaking its fur, flicking its tail. But then it arrives, strolling into the room with maddening grace, and I remember — all over again — the slippered paws gripping against my throat, the way I hacked and wheezed by the Christmas tree.

The demon stays firmly by the side of its human, practicing a quick roll-over, a move I mastered many years ago. Overall, though, its routine is stronger — more expertly choreographed. More stylish. As I watch, I wait for the baring of its teeth, the sharp gleam of its incisors. Maybe it senses that there are too many people around, too many potential witnesses.

The humans think it is a good dog.

Noodles tries to refocus me. She nips at my neck, nudges me with her nose. Her legs are so short that when she dances, it's barely noticeable; but she's always moving, always a slick blur across the room. "Noodles . . . does her own thing," her human says, which Max tells me is code for "Noodles hasn't *learned* a thing." Her obedience is dreadful. Her tricks, nonexistent. I'm leaps and bounds ahead of her.

Elvis, on the other hand, is progressing masterfully; his turns are crisp, his jumps high. And while I'm trying not to think of him as competition, the thought does occur to me—that to win the walk-on movie role, Max and I will have to dance more skillfully than every dog in this room.

At some point, Greta turns down the music. She's wearing a Christmas sweater that frightens me; two googly eyes peer at us, wild like the sheepdog's. "All right!" she says. "I hope you all had a nice holiday! Almost in the new year, now. That means we're going to ramp up the pace and start putting all these moves together. You should be building your choreography and thinking a lot about artistry. One of the big things I always teach is walking backward. Some dogs really don't take to this, especially when doing it on command. But let's go ahead and give it a try. Places!"

Elvis and I line up with the other dogs, shoulder to shoulder in a large circle. Together, we learn our new hand cue. The trick itself is more difficult. I try to walk backward as if I were born to do so, as if I have never walked any other way. But I'm so desperate to impress

Max, to keep up the momentum we've built, that my legs refuse to move in the right direction.

We try over.

And over.

And over.

"It's okay," Max tells me, his palms gently cupping my ears.

But it isn't! It's the first trick I've stumbled over! If I just had a few more moments, to work it out in my head, to grasp the logic of it . . .

"He might be hitting a wall," Uncle Reggie says. "He's made so much progress. It makes sense that he's going to trip up with something."

The sheepdog is all I can think. It mocks me from the corner of the room, quiet laughter rumbling from its furry gut. And I realize, in a flash of great understanding, that I lost something in the battle with my miniature foe. As the wiry demon clung to my throat, it was stealing everything it could: my energy, my focus. It takes, and it takes, and it takes. Now everything feels just a little worse. And it worries me.

Dogs in movies should be able to walk backward.

A few days before New Year's, Uncle Reggie folds the blanket on our couch for the last time. I'm sad that I have no more bacon to share with him before he leaves, packing his nice-smelling shirts into a stiff suitcase. I lick his ears. The brown skin of his wrists. "I know, I know," he says. "But I'm really not going that far."

I've been listening to my family—and they've told me that Uncle Reggie got a job training dogs, right here in town. He bought a piece of land with maple trees and a small yellow house, and Max and I are welcome there, any time we want. "Seriously," he tells us as the car backs away. "*Any* time."

I know it should feel like the beginning of something. I trust Uncle Reggie and believe we will see him again. But a part of me wonders if this is also an ending, if our early mornings in the cul-de-sac are only a memory now. I am already longing for them: learning trick after trick, paws in the air, bodies against the cool grass.

Humans have so many ways to see one another, with their cars and their buses, their opposable thumbs that easily open doors; they can leave the house any time they want, visit any time it pleases them. I have never known that kind of freedom, and this has taught me patience: I must wait by the door, head on my paws, ears cocked to the sound of footsteps.

I already miss Uncle Reggie's footsteps.

He waves goodbye from his seat in the car—and for the next few days I spend half my time on the couch, resting my jaw on his blanket, so that his scent is still with us. The house feels strange without him. In the evenings, to distract myself, I dig several small holes in the yard and crunch every pinecone that I can find, sharply, with my back teeth. "Where are you even getting these?" Max says, brushing out pinecone shards from beneath his bed. But I think he understands. I think he is out of sorts, too.

It's almost a relief when New Year's Eve arrives, even though it is the second worst night of the year. Great balls of fiery blue burst in the sky, and the air trembles worse than a thunderstorm. All throughout the neighborhood, dogs howl. Any night with fireworks, I feel a greater kinship with my canine friends, as our voices ring out and become one. The only voice missing is the sheepdog's. It does not bark. I can only assume that something in its coat renders it immune to the noises of the night.

That evening, Emmaline knocks on Max's door, waking us both. We've fallen asleep with our heads together, dreaming of the movies.

"Max?" she says.

Max's eyes are still closed. He grumbles. "Yeah?"

"Mommy wants to know if you still want to go to the party tonight at the scary lady's house."

"I'm pretty tired, Em."

"*Pleeease?* Can you please come? There are going to be cupcakes!"

It's nice to know that Max is like me — he wants to make Emmaline happy; I know this because he pushes down the sheets and laces his shoes, and soon we are out the door. A tub of turkey chili sloshes in Mom's hands as the five of us trot into the cul-de-sac. The night may be young, or the night may be old — I still haven't grasped the expression — but either way, it's brisk. The moon illuminates the sky.

"What's Uncle Reggie doing tonight?" Max asks.

"I think he's going to a party in his neighborhood," Mom says. She's wearing her head wrap again, the one with the stars. "But you can call him later, if you want. I'm sure he'd like to hear from you."

Dad stares down at me. "Are you *positive* it's all right with Cynthia that we're bringing Cosmo?"

Mom shrugs. "She told me to bring him so he'd keep Boo busy."

"I just don't know anyone else who'd bring a dog to a party."

Max steps in. "But Cosmo's the perfect guest. Aren't you, boy?"

Truthfully, I haven't been to many parties, but on the way to the scary lady's house, I am on my best behavior. Hers is the second on our street: a dark gray bungalow with white shutters, and large cracks in the driveway that Emmaline hops over. They have squirrel bushes, too, although they are smaller, with less space to shove your head between branches. Noises thump from inside the house.

Max rings the bell. Almost immediately, the scary lady opens the door.

"You came!" she bellows at us, swaying slightly in a sparkly dress. Her scent is overpowering—rubber and roses—and her claws are always terrifyingly long.

Tonight she has painted them blue. "I'm so happy you came! Eric! Eric, look who's here! And you brought chili! I do *love* chili, HA-HA-HA! Come in, come in."

Max, Emmaline, and I are quickly shuffled into her backyard, a wonderland of pine trees and dropped toys. I catch Boo's scent everywhere—on the tips of grass, in spots throughout the yard. But where is he? Inside?

I don't have to wonder for long.

Someone shouts, "Incoming!" And there is Boo, the German shorthaired pointer, bursting out the side door, knocking over a tray of food, crashing headfirst into a plastic garden gnome. Unfazed, he sprints figure eights around the flower beds before diving at my feet, rolling over, and exposing his belly. Looking up at me, he smiles with his eyes, the way only dogs can.

Hello there, he says.

And I lick his muzzle in reply.

After a while, more kids begin to filter into the backyard, and we play astronauts. This is a wonderful game that involves wandering slowly around the grass and pretending that you are in space. I take to it instantly; at heart, I am a dreamer.

Boo pants wildly when the fireworks start, shaking and howling. I find myself joining in, until Max drapes his arm around me. "It's okay," he says, running his fingers through the soft fur of my bib. "Nothing bad's happening. I'm here."

The sky splinters, our faces lighting up with glow. All around us is a steady *BOOM, BOOM, BOOM.*

Max remains, unshakable. I would like to tell him that he is brave and wise and strong. So I nudge my face into his, over and over, until the message becomes clear: *You are brilliant, you are, you are.*

"Max?" Emmaline says, sliding next to us. "I can't find Mommy and Daddy."

"I'm sure they're somewhere inside."

"But I *can't find* them."

Max drapes his free arm around her. "Okay, hang out with us for a while."

Emmaline kicks the sides of her sneakers together, watches them bounce apart.

"I miss Uncle Reggie."

Max tells her, "Yeah. Me, too. But we'll still see him a lot . . . I think."

"Like at the dance club?"

Max nods.

And Emmaline says, very quietly, "Can I come? I can help you win your movie."

I'm cowering from the large *bang*s in the sky, but my tail still flips back and forth. I hadn't considered this: how Emmaline could help our training. Yet she is excellent in so many areas. Her cartwheels are exceptional. When she runs, she is extraordinarily quick—and she is also quick to forgive. Once, many summers ago, Emmaline presented me with a firefly crawling up her hand. "It's good luck," she told me. "A good-luck firefly." I ate it. I ate it and Emmaline cried. But later that day, she let me run through the sprinkler next to her, and we laughed with our bellies as I shook out my wet fur. Emmaline is a special human.

Max must sense my thoughts, because he says, "I'd like that."

Above us, fireworks pop. We watch the rest of them side by side.

"Long time no see," Uncle Reggie says, wrapping his arms around Max and Emmaline. "What's it been, a week and a half?"

I wait patiently by their feet, until it's my turn. With certain people, I never expose my underside; I feel too open, too vulnerable. But with Uncle Reggie, the movement comes naturally. I spin over on the soft bed of the community center's lawn, my back legs splayed, my stomach to the air, and he bends down for several long pats.

"He remembers about twenty tricks," Max says. "So we've got, like, half the choreography down? He still can't walk backward for more than two steps, though. I've been working with him every day, but his legs get all tangled."

"We can fix that," Uncle Reggie says. I notice that his shoes smell of other dogs and are hairy at the toes: clumps of fur clinging to the edges. "We'll have a big training session today."

"I'm helping," Emmaline says proudly, her hands clasped behind her back.

"Glad to have you on board," Uncle Reggie tells her, and then smiles down at me. "Ready, goober?"

Goober. Max calls me goober occasionally, and silly dog. Humans and their nicknames—I just don't understand them sometimes. Max has so many nicknames, from family and friends (Maximus, Maximilian, Maxwell, sweetie, sweetheart, honey, kiddo, buddy, champ), but to me, he is just Max. Always Max. I love the simplicity of it, the short sound. I can imagine saying it out loud.

I tell everyone that I am ready.

The community center smells strange today—and I realize it's because the sheepdog is already here. I spot it across the room, mud speckles on its paws. This is alarming in and of itself: there is no mud outside! So how are the edges of its fur crusted with dirt? It must have conjured the mud out of nowhere, or woken

up early and romped darkly through the woods, when the dirt patches are still slick with dew. As I flounce through the door, the sheepdog refuses to catch my eye—the arrogance of it, the *nerve* of it. When the sheepdog bows to its human, it flaps its ears wildly, side to side, as if attempting to fly.

Noodles is on the other side of the room, chasing her stubby tail, and I'm afraid—on her behalf—that she'll never catch it. Sometimes tails are tricky, with minds of their own, and they remain *slightly* out of reach, no matter how fast you spin. But she continues with her quest, ignoring her human, who's trying to command her to march. Noodles still hasn't mastered a single trick—not the hop, or the weave, or the bow—but this doesn't seem to faze her. She smiles frequently, the tip of her tongue sticking out, just beyond her overbite.

Especially by comparison, Elvis and Oliver are speeding along with their routine. Elvis is no longer second-guessing himself; he's becoming more and more fearless. His moves are crisper than mine, more—

Wait!

The sheepdog's brought a toy today, a plush alligator with googly eyes. I wonder if this could be the sheepdog's Achilles' heel. Every break between dance moves, the sheepdog nudges the toy—mouths it, picks it up, shakes it. Perhaps Noodles is thinking what I'm thinking, because she makes a break for it: swiftly lunging for the toy, skittering away on short legs. The alligator is almost the size of her head; it dangles from her mouth. And for a second, guilt creeps in. How would I feel if Mr. Oinkers was kidnapped?

"Okay," Uncle Reggie says, as Noodles darts past him. "Besides the reverse walk, let's go over what we've got. Emmaline, you let us know what you think."

Emmaline gives us a thumbs-up.

Focusing, taking my cue, I lift my paw in the air, bouncing to the best of my ability. Max starts feeding me commands—*turn, left, right, bow.* Shuffling to the side, my front legs cross as Max grapevines beside me. When I march in place, I curl each paw with precision, and drop to a roll immediately afterward. On my back, there's a moment or two when the pain arrives, crawling up my spine. I feel my age; I feel every year I have ever lived. Then I recover, wriggling back to a stand. I'm not sure what comes over me, but I begin to improvise, boldly adding my own moves. I channel Danny's confidence in *Grease.* I channel Sandy's passion. Suddenly, my legs have minds of their own, and I am leaping, the ground beneath my paws floating away.

"Huh," Uncle Reggie says. "He got about an inch off the floor. That's . . . Well, he's got spirit. I'll give him that."

"An *inch*," Max says. "An inch off the floor."

For whatever reason, my family begins to laugh. Did someone make a joke? I don't usually get human jokes, unless they involve the misfortune of chickens, but Max is very, very funny. *Why are playing cards like wolves,* he once asked me. *They come in packs!* I concentrated so hard on understanding the joke that I began to sneeze — and then it clicked. *Packs!* Genius! I chuckled to myself for an entire night and continued to do so throughout the rest of the week, whenever the brilliance of it struck me again.

"That's about all we have," Max finally says, scratching his head. "Those are all the basics, at least. How was it, Em?"

Emmaline cocks her head to the side, a gesture I still don't wholly understand. "I . . . I like it."

"But?" Max says.

"It's just . . . it needs *more*. Like when you and Mommy and Daddy and I used to dance." She starts shyly skipping around, her arms flapping with delicate energy. "You know?"

Max sighs a long sigh. "You're right. She's right,

Uncle Reggie. We need some bigger moves. Or maybe just one really, really big move."

With the tip of her shoe, Emmaline traces a circle in the grass. "Max? I think you need to be more a part of it, too."

No one speaks for a moment. We all know what she means, even though Max won't like to admit it. Yes, he's feeding me the hand cues and treats, but he's dancing without heart. I am carrying us.

Uncle Reggie says, "I hate to say it, buddy, but she has a point. In the competition, you're going to be the focus just as much as Cosmo. The judges are going to score you both. Bigger moves are a plus: maybe an actual jump, if he can manage it? But it also comes down to *you* conveying emotions, letting us really feel the dance." Uncle Reggie bends his knees, lowering to my level. His hands cup my muzzle. "Remember that you and Cosmo have each other's backs. If you're feeling nervous, lean on him when you have to."

On the way to Uncle Reggie's house for a snack, I repeat that advice, telling Max, *Lean on me, because we need this movie role.* We cannot be apart—so I'll be strong for both of us.

I'm not sure how I pictured the inside of Uncle Reggie's house, or if I pictured it at all. But when we

park the car and venture inside, I see a couch like ours, and a comfortable rug with cushioning beneath it. As in Max's room, pictures hang on the walls, but instead of astronauts, they're jazz musicians.

"Miles Davis and Charlie Parker," Uncle Reggie says, pointing at the posters like he's introducing us to old friends. And then, in the kitchen: "Water? Juice? Chocolate milk?"

Emmaline and Max say *chocolate milk* at the same time. They mix their drinks, swirling in the dark syrup, and I watch, knowing I shouldn't want the milk, but wanting it anyway. In the garage, they set their glasses on a miniature fridge, and Uncle Reggie switches on the overhead lights that blink and blink.

"I know it's not a true dance studio or anything," he says, gazing around, "but I thought we could practice in here when we're not at the club and it's too cold to dance outside."

It is beautiful, I say, and I would know; I have seen the inside of many garages. (You'd be surprised how many people believe this is the only place for dogs.) So I can tell you how bare this is: no tennis rackets, no exercise machines, no old toys stacked against the walls. Humans have so much *stuff,* things that pile up and up. There is something wonderful about the openness; in here, anything is possible.

Emmaline flings out her arms and twirls around.

"Oh, man," Max says, "it's perfect."

"Glad you think so." Uncle Reggie smiles, peering down at me. "What do you say, goober? Any more energy left for some big moves?"

The truth is, no. The dance club this morning has exhausted me more than usual, and I would like to stay very still, a hand massaging the scruff of my neck. The couch at home is calling me: the soft leather, the deep slots between the cushions. But I don't want to disappoint them, and they're right: Since the grand prize is a film role, the judges will look for a *wow* factor, a showstopper—a move that will leave them in awe. Max is depending on me. So I creak to a stand and wag my tail as fast as I can muster.

With Emmaline's help, we consider several big moves. "What if," she says, crouching down on her hands and knees, "Cosmo bows, and keeps his front legs out like this, but his back legs go round and round?" She demonstrates, circling the floor.

"Hmm," Max says. "Is that big enough?"

"I've got an idea," Uncle Reggie says. "We can incorporate that, Em, but maybe we should also try that

jump. Definitely not a big jump, based on his age, but Max—if you get on your knees, bend to the side, and hold your arm out. That's it. A little lower . . . Good. You think he can hurdle that?"

Max judges the distance between his arm and the ground. "Maybe."

We start slow, Max guiding me over little obstacles around the garage. From the backyard, Uncle Reggie grabs a few sticks with the bark still on, and I focus on leaping over them, stretching my legs as far as they can go. On TV once, I saw greyhounds on a track, their bodies straight from toes to tail, and I think about being *long* and *fast* and *strong*. Max is striving, too. His wrists flick; he stoops with energy, leads me with heart. And every time I hurdle a stick, Emmaline holds out a chicken treat in her palm. "Yay," she keeps telling me, even though I'm barely jumping at all. "You're so good, Cosmo."

"One last time?" Max asks me, before we head into the kitchen.

One last time.

I hop again, throwing all of myself into the move. But I stumble, leaping too hard, my left paw bending against the cool concrete. Immediately, a jagged pain works its way up my leg. From the outside, it looks like I've recovered nicely—because I hold it in: the whimper that wants to escape me, the yawn I'd like to calm myself with. We've come so far, to end our practice this way.

Max wrinkles his forehead. "You all right, Cosmo?"

I am fine, I tell him, hiding my limp. *Just fine.*

By the refrigerator, I lap up water like I've never *tasted* water, like this is the last drink I'll ever have. The liquid sloshes, dripping from my muzzle, wetting my whiskers. I don't want anyone to see me crash this way, panting while trying to ignore the pain in my paw, but I barely make it past the hallway before I collapse. My paws slide out from under me. To save face, I smile with my tongue hanging. *That was intentional,* I say to the room. *Everything is fine.*

Uncle Reggie believes my show. "What we need now," he says, "is a song."

We watch *Grease* in front of his couch, our paws bare on the carpet. Emmaline lies on her stomach, hands underneath her chin, brown eyes staring up at the TV. It flickers. And when Danny and Sandy come on-screen, I picture Max and me, dancing like them. Dancing bigger than life, on the set of a movie: us, inseparable, together.

Uncle Reggie points at Sandy, who—I realize

now—is undeniably part golden retriever. Consider her fur (pale yellow, like mine), her good-natured disposition, and the way she swishes.

"How about 'Summer Nights'?" Uncle Reggie asks.

Max grimaces. "That's so . . . romantic."

"Too awkward, then?"

"*Way* too awkward. Same with 'Hopelessly Devoted to You' and 'You're the One That I Want.' The song needs to be . . . I don't know. I'll know it when I hear it."

The last scene takes place at a school carnival, after Danny and Sandy circle each other, as dogs would, and make declarations of love. Sandy has already said the movie's most famous words: "Tell me about it, Stud." This line has always meant a great deal to me. According to the man who changed the cardboard boxes when I was a puppy, Stud was my father's name.

As I listen to the final song, "We Go Together," I feel as if I'm truly understanding it for the first time. Sandy, Danny, and the rest of their group—they belong with one another, no matter how time and circumstances threaten to tear them apart. Friends go with friends. Family goes with family. The music wraps around us, upbeat and blissful.

"You know what?" Max says. "This would be a good song."

The rest of the choreography falls into place after that. Over the next couple of days, we add some extra nods to the scene: Max snapping his fingers as I point my nose to the sky, the two of us prancing like we're at the fair. And I remind myself that I have the soul of a dancer; my legs will go where my heart tells them to go—even if my injured paw is aching. It's gotten so bad that I've started to swallow the vitamins Mom gives me in the morning, instead of shoving them in the crack by the fridge.

One night before bed, Max asks, "Cosmo, are you limping?"

I let the facade slip, and it won't happen again. Max shouldn't worry that my injury will affect our dance, that it will slide the movie role out of our reach. I climb the small stairs onto Max's bed, by myself, without so much as a whimper.

"I just want you to know," Max says, putting aside his laptop, "dancing like this isn't a science. I know we're going for the big prize and there's a lot at stake . . . but it doesn't have to be perfect. *You* don't have to be perfect."

I shove Mr. Oinkers under my good paw, listening to him squeak wildly, letting his sound fill the room—because I noticed something today. There are

new blankets on the couch, and they smell like Dad. His hairs are on the couch pillows; the cushions are taking his shape. Right now, in the kitchen, he's fighting with Mom. I hear their voices rise higher. Kitchen cabinets slam.

No more chasing balls in the house, I tell myself, or climbing onto the couch. No more barking at reckless squirrels in the bushes. I'll save my energy for dancing and only dancing—because I remember my promise to Max, to love him doggedly, to always remain by his side. I see it, too: Max's focus, Max's bravery. The way we are holding on when everything feels like it's crumbling apart.

I will be perfect, I tell him with my eyes. *For you, I will.*

Late in January, the most wonderful thing happens.
White fluff begins to fall from the sky. Snow is rare
in North Carolina. Our winters are usually marked
with crisp, bright days and only a touch of rain. Snow
always feels like a big event.

"Do you think it'll stick?" Max asks me on Monday
evening. The two of us are perched by the dance club's
windows, watching flakes float slowly onto the frozen
ground. His voice is airy with hope. In response to his
question, I snort a trail of snot across the glass, but
otherwise I don't answer him. I've learned not to offer
opinions about things I will never understand.

Oliver pops his head next to us. *"Please,* no school."

Max crosses his fingers in the air.

"I have a quiz tomorrow," Oliver says. "On a book I haven't read. And I'd rather build an ice cave with Elvis."

"I don't think he'd be very helpful," Max says—and I'm surprised how quickly his response comes, how the words flow so smoothly from his mouth. "Ice-cave building . . . You kind of need hands."

Elvis is oblivious to the snow. We are supposed to be learning how to weave between our humans' legs, but he's preoccupied with sniffing my injured paw. *Ignore it,* I say, as concern folds across his forehead. He licks the webbing between my toes, and this worries me even more—because if he can smell it, sense it, how bad is my injury? How bad is it, really?

Overall, Elvis and I are progressing step for step, like we're walking the same path. Oliver and Max compare choreography, chat quietly about the day of the competition—it seems so far away, doesn't it? But it'll sneak up on us, if we're not careful. It's certainly sneaking up on Noodles, who's barely learned a thing.

All the while, as we practice and talk, the sheepdog dances darkly in the corner, perfectly nailing "walk backward," and I vow once more: *I will be better. Just wait.*

Afterward, we pack into our cars as the snow falls, and I wish I could stick my head out the window and chomp at the floating clumps. I don't sleep much that night. I pick at the tufts of fur on my bad paw, hoping to extract the pain, hoping that this won't harm us—me and Max, both. In this condition, can I physically perform the big move? How much will it harm our movie chances?

"Can't sleep?" Max says, deep in the night.

I wonder if he's been awake all this time, thinking what I'm thinking, too.

The following morning, school *is* canceled. *Canceled!* Putting my weight on my good side, I follow Max as he skips around the kitchen, whooping and hollering with his arms in the air. "Yes, yes, *yes!*" Emmaline is excited, too. She and Max grip hands, spinning on the spot. I try to join them, but halfway through my first spin, I wince and jolt—and almost knock Emmaline to the ground. She giggles at me and says, "Cosmo, *snow!*" Which is almost as good as: *Cosmo, cookie!*

The happiness is overwhelming. The three of us cannot stop panting with joy.

Mom and Dad slide their way into the kitchen, Dad saying, "Looks like you got lucky." Mom turns on the coffeepot and says a very simple "Morning." I notice a chill between them—Dad slept on the couch again last night—but I'm distracted. The snow! No school! A whole extra day with Max!

"Here's a thought," Dad says. "I'm gonna shovel the sidewalks so Cosmo can go out, but after that . . . sledding?"

"Sledding!" Emmaline echoes.

"I'm up for it," Max says.

In all honesty, I'm not entirely sure how I will navigate the snow this year. Typically, the cold stiffens my joints, and I am wary of ice.

Several winters ago, I slipped on a patch of black ice, the kind that's impossible to see until you are already sliding. I remember slamming against the ground and crying out with a moan then a howl. My leg—it was in a unique pain, sharp and all-consuming.

Max, who was walking right by my side, dropped to his knees and yelled, "Dad!" I was telling Max, *I'm glad it was me, I'm glad it wasn't you, you need your limbs much more than I do,* when Dad came bursting out of the garage. Within seconds, he appraised the situation, wrapping his fingers lightly around my foreleg. "I think it might be broken. *Shhh, shhh,* Cosmo, it's okay, buddy. Try not to move. Max, go get your mom and tell her to start the car. Get some blankets, too."

He lifted me softly, like I was a plush toy: practically weightless. I wore a cast for a month, and spent my time laid out on the couch, watching bad daytime TV. I could afford that luxury, then.

But not now. Not when we are months away from our chance at the movie role, from proving that Max and I belong together.

Half of the worry evaporates after Max bundles in three layers (sweater, scarf, coat), and we rush outside into the whiteness, snowflakes on our eyelashes. I feel *terrific*. In a previous life, I may have been a husky. The cooler air agrees with me. Ignoring my injury, I tear around in wild circles, faster, *faster,* as fast as I can. For a few precious seconds, I feel like a puppy again. Then comes a dull ache in my hips, and even more pain in my paw—but it's worth it, to be happy with Emmaline and Max in that pure, indefinable way.

I chew on a ball of snow and stop myself from rolling in several intriguing patches on the ground. There are many scents that I would happily roll in, given the opportunity, but over the years I've grasped that most of them are frowned upon. On ten or twelve occasions, I have been given a bath immediately afterward. Baths seem like a form of punishment, with water that slicks down your tail, and suds that creep between the pads of your paws. You will never feel like a proper dog when you smell of coconut shampoo.

The light grows brighter. Max and I make snow angels in the cul-de-sac, our bodies pressed into the soft fluff. His angel is neat and tidy. Mine, as Dad says, is "wild and unpredictable." Next to us, Emmaline builds a snow-human with twigs and a carrot stick, both of which I am tempted to chew.

"Want it?" Emmaline asks, handing me the longest twig. "I'll share."

I do want it, very much, and Max and I end up playing tug-of-war until the twig snaps.

Dad begins fumbling in the garage. We hear a variety of noises until he emerges, lugging a strange narrow boat behind him. "Thought the kayak might work," he declares.

The hill by our house is already crowded with kids, sledding on cardboard boxes and inside recycling bins. Our boat is the star. Max seems very proud. He races up the hill and down again—up and down, up and down, over and over.

Here is what I know: In my younger days, I would

have bounded after him. My paws would've kicked up snow, my tongue draping to the side. I would've pulled the canoe like a sled dog. Now I watch Max, and I wait for him. At the bottom of the hill, each time, he ruffles my head and asks, "How you doing, Cosmo, huh?"

After several hours, Max is visibly slower climbing up the hill. "Just one more," he tries to convince Dad.

"Come on," Dad says. "It's lunchtime, and your toes must be freezing."

Emmaline adds, "Daddy, I lost my mitten."

Max wipes his nose on the sleeve of his jacket. "Just a minute longer?"

"Kiddo," Dad says, "I'm sorry. We can come back after lunch if you really want to."

Max looks down at me, like he knows I'll understand. And in that moment, I do. I really do. Max doesn't want to go back inside, because everything is better out here. There is snow out here. And fun out here. And no fighting out here. If I were him, if I could, I'd run right back up the hill.

Instead, we turn for home.

Back inside, I expect Mom to greet us. Max has previously explained that Mom's hot chocolate is the best. On the coldest days, she makes it with all milk instead of water. She whisks the milk until it's frothy. I can't have chocolate, but I still think about all the food lovingly prepared for me: Biscuits at birthdays. Jerky snacks on car trips. Little things count.

This time, Mom doesn't leave her room. So Max stands on his toes and whisks the milk. "Love you," he says as he hands the hot chocolate to Emmaline. We used to be the type of family that said *I love you* constantly. We passed out *I love you*s like cookies. It strikes me that Mom and Dad haven't said it to each other for a long, long time.

"Sometimes I think that you and I should run away together," Max tells me that evening, when we are alone. "I . . . I don't *really* mean that. But let's just . . . Can we just imagine it for a second? Like, we could live in a tree house. Or a cave! Or how about on the beach? You like the beach." He scoots down from his bed and lies with me on the floor. "I could bring my rocket supplies and we could spend all day building things, and then at night we could just hang out and look at the stars and stuff."

The idea does have its appeal.

But I still whimper, half because my paw aches, half to express my disapproval. I like it *here*.

"I know," he says. "I know. I just wish . . . I just wish

I could . . ." He trails off, eyes on the ceiling. I want to tell him that, whatever he wishes, he can achieve. I want to tell him that he is the brilliant spark in my ordinary life. He is stronger than he knows.

So I press my snout into his belly.

He sits up, says I'm a good dog, a very good dog.

We wrap a blanket around our shoulders, and together stare into the growing darkness.

Winter doesn't last long. It feels as if I've barely blinked before it's gone. And then: the quick slide into spring, the wonderfully named dogwood trees exploding into bloom. I can't even step outside without sneezing. Pollen constantly crawls into my nose.

And through it all, we dance. We dance before dinner, as Mom boils spaghetti in the kitchen. We dance in Uncle Reggie's garage, pretending that we are on the set of a film. Almost all of the choreography we know perfectly: the dipping and bowing, the marching and hopping. I even nail the backward walk. And yet, I can't help but think that our routine lacks pizzazz.

The Movie People will require pizzazz.

"It's still *missing* something," Max keeps saying. "You know?"

Uncle Reggie says not to worry; the club will continue to give us "pointers." I find this confusing. There are no German shorthaired pointers here.

One Saturday morning, Noodles escapes from the room, her human flailing after her. In their wake is pure quiet. We are so absorbed in our own worlds. Elvis and Oliver are practicing their big move (Oliver drops to his hands and knees as Elvis climbs on his back), while the sheepdog is—

The sheepdog is balancing on its hind legs!

I blink, wondering if my eyes are deceiving me. But no. It stands tall, belly exposed; that plush alligator swings from its mouth, taunting me. Unlike everyone else, except Noodles, our big move isn't progressing half as well. When Max dips his arm, my back legs always catch.

Max groans. "This is my fault. We should have picked something else, something easier."

"Hey," Uncle Reggie says. "He'll get it. Just give him time."

I try to listen to his words, and picture us at the dance competition—then us *winning* the competition, strutting onto that movie set, triumphant and together.

Sometime in March, all the dogs in the neighborhood start shedding their winter coats. The humans barely notice it, but in the streets there are golden hairs and white zigzags, drifting in the wind. For the most part, the weeks tick by.

Until that hurricane feeling returns. Dad is still sleeping on the couch, and the living room is starting to seem like *his* room. He leaves his shoes under the coffee table and his books by the lamp. At night, I whimper by the back door, even though I don't really need to go out; I just want to do *something* — sniff around or rub my face in the dirt, anything to focus my mind.

One of those nights, Dad opens the sliding-glass door and says, "Be good, Cosmo. I'm gonna watch the game, so just go potty and come back in, okay?" Then I'm alone in the backyard, the smell of garbage in the air. *Garbage day,* I think — when the leftover pizza boxes, banana peels, and chicken trimmings are discarded into a bin and wheeled to the edge of the driveway. Humans love garbage day. Neighbors stream from their houses and greet one another with mutual respect, waving and joking about the heaviness of the bins, all the wonderful things inside.

The bushes smell of garbage, too.

I hear a rustling in them. My ears pivot back. *What's this?*

Almost immediately, a cat pops from between the branches. His face is narrower than any cat I know, with sharp whiskers that glance off my snout as he jumps. A strong, earthy smell wafts from him, not unlike the trash. He begins rubbing against me, his nose to my legs. *My,* I tell him, *aren't you a friendly fellow!* It's been a long time since I've met a cat so eager to cuddle.

Something flickers in my mind. Something just doesn't seem *right* about him. But I'm so preoccupied with smelling his backside, trying to pinpoint his scent, that nothing can deter me.

Doing my best to remember how to communicate with cats (Should I bow? Yip?), I beckon him through the open door. I assume that we'll gleefully romp around the living room, as Boo and I do. Maybe a gentle game of tug-of-war is in the cards? Emmaline is already asleep, and Max is in bed, reading about astronauts. So whatever activity we choose, it must be quiet.

The cat sniffs the cabinets. He rolls over on his back and wiggles his little legs in the air. Suddenly,

Mom rounds the corner of the kitchen. "Cosmo, what are you—?" Her words cut off. And then she screams.

I realize, all at once, that I've been fooled.

In retrospect, I saw the clues; I just couldn't assemble them in any meaningful way. I've witnessed raccoons before in their native environments. Once, on a camping trip, a pair of them darted onto our picnic table, stole half of Max's peanut butter and jelly sandwich, and scampered back into the woods with devilish delight.

The cat is not a cat!

It startles me just how wrong I was.

"Oh my goodness!" Mom shouts as the raccoon darts between her ankles. She hops onto the countertop, legs swinging in space. "*Ooooh* my goodness. No-no-no-*no*! David, get in here!"

"What's going on with—?" Dad says, swiftly entering the kitchen. He smells freshly bathed. Like Mom, his words stop midsentence and begin again: "Holy cow!"

"Don't just stand there!" Mom shouts. "Get the broom! Help me shoo it out."

"Jeez, I hope it doesn't have rabies."

"*David!*"

"Right. Broom, broom."

I sense the urgency in their voices, although for the life of me I can't unravel the reason for their panic. There are no sandwiches around for the raccoon to snatch—not even a cheese stick. We are in no danger.

I approach the little critter. Sometimes a smell is so intriguing that I want to be *inside* it. Sometimes I sniff and sniff but cannot get enough, so I am forced to nose-dive, throwing my whole body into the scent, coating myself in its glorious aroma. I do that with the raccoon's muddy footprints, which track halfway across the kitchen.

"Cosmo!" Mom is saying to me, her hands fluttering through the air. "Get away from it! Max's room! Go to Max's room!"

You're right, I think. *Max needs to see this.* It is a stroke of luck that he appears at the kitchen door just as Dad returns triumphantly with the broom. "Whoa," Max says, Emmaline next to him. She's heard the noises and woken up. How fortunate!

Dad jumps quickly in front of them. "Max, go put your little sister back to bed, *now.*"

"Daddy," Emmaline says. "Can we keep him, please? *Pleeease?*"

"ENOUGH!" Mom shouts, snatching the broom

from Dad and pushing the raccoon gently outside. The critter scurries off into the night. "Max, Emmaline, Cosmo, back to bed."

In the hours afterward, Mom and Dad scrub the floors, slapping the mop against the tile. They snap at each other.

Out of my way.

Why'd you do that?

No, the towels are over there.

Where?

There!

It gets so bad that Max covers his ears. And I wonder if the sheepdog was behind this, if the raccoon was sent to trick me, to identify our weaknesses. I turn over on my plush bed, Mr. Oinkers beneath me. Am I losing my touch? Intimidating the outdoor animals is part of my job. Who am I, if not protector of the house?

There's a soft knock at the door. It's Emmaline. She doesn't want to be by herself—not now, not with the angry voices. The two of them lift me into Max's bed, and we settle into the warmth and the cushions, and pretend. *We do not hear them.* We do not.

And I feel guilty. Because wasn't this my fault? Didn't I invite the raccoon in?

"Hey, Cosmo," Max says, his sleepy hand reaching over to pat my head. The corner of his mouth inches up. "That raccoon? I know you were just trying to make a friend."

I close my eyes and tell myself that dancing can still keep us together.

At first, the cloudiness goes away if I blink very, very slowly. But soon my eyes begin to feel glassy, like I'm looking at the world through a water dish.

"He's missing some of the hand cues," Uncle Reggie says, scratching the back of his neck. We're at the dance club on a drizzly afternoon, and the same sensation has plagued me the whole day: that the sheepdog is stalking me, right over my shoulder, right where I cannot see. And Max's hands! They're moving so fast. They're fluttering, half-blurred. Is he telling me to lift my right paw, or my left?

"I just don't understand," Max says. "He *knows* these."

Oliver scrunches his mouth. "Well . . . I don't know, dude. Sometimes Elvis forgets things, too."

But right now, Elvis is shining. He's bowing so precisely, floating through his routine. Even Noodles is surpassing me today. *Noodles!* She manages to lift her front paws to a beat—the first trick I've ever seen her do.

Days later, when the dark spots begin to stay in my vision, Mom brings me to the vet, who declares it a wonder that I can see at all. "He's an old dog with old eyes," the vet says. "He's happy, though. You can tell he's happy."

On the way back in the car, it hits me: That's why I thought the raccoon was a cat! My eyesight—it's failing.

I am failing.

From then on, I take extra measures to make sure I'm getting things right. I triple-check with my nose, my paws, my ears. Is this *really* Mr. Oinkers, or is it someone else's pig? Is *this* the spot I peed on last week? At the dance club, I follow Max's hand cues with extra care, relying more and more on memory.

And I start to question whether my eyesight is the only thing deteriorating. There's my arthritis and the pain in my paw—I know that. But what's worse is my ears. They used to prick at everything. I could hear the crackle of chicken in a skillet, two houses away. I could tell when our neighbor was running water for a bath. And I used to lift my leg fully to urinate, after storing my resources all day to mark lampposts, bushes, trees. Now I tilt my head all the way to listen. My leg barely drifts off the ground.

It's embarrassing.

More than that, the sheepdog isn't experiencing any pain. It's young. It catches hand signals as they're given. Elvis and Noodles help where they can, providing encouragement when I nail a move, but I wonder if they see it, too: that the sheepdog is winning. That it's getting closer and closer to finishing what it started in the park, all those years ago—separating Max and me.

"You all right, bud?" Uncle Reggie asks on the morning of Emmaline's birthday. It is one of those unseasonably hot days, the sky a cloudless blue, and I'm lying very, very still on the driveway.

Uncle Reggie helps me to my feet—with my paw, I'm having trouble standing today—and inside, Mom makes strawberry pancakes for breakfast. Even though it isn't *my* birthday, I chomp through several, and Emmaline, Max, and I watch cartoons until heading to Sawyer Park.

"You remembered the balloons, right?" Mom asks Dad on the way there.

"I thought you were grabbing the balloons," he says.

"Chill," Max groans. "I have them. See?" He lifts a bag out of his backpack, filled with many colors.

"And the plastic forks?" Mom asks.

"Got 'em," Uncle Reggie says.

Dad taps the steering wheel. "Everything's going to be fine. It's just a birthday party."

"Well, it's *your daughter's* birthday party," Mom bites back. "So it matters a bit more . . ."

Uncle Reggie pats Mom on the shoulder. "Let's just enjoy the day."

Everyone sighs, except Emmaline, who giddily reminds us that she is six. Six! How'd that happen so quickly? I remember years ago, when she was small, and I would pull her wagon as if I were a horse. On the kitchen wall there are pencil marks, tracking our heights. The lowest one is mine: COSMO, AGE 13. Even Emmaline is taller than me now.

As my family exits the car and begins blowing up balloons beneath the gazebo, I patrol the perimeter. No sheepdog. I'd be able to smell the demon if it were here. There are tall grasses, though—along with lost

Frisbees, Popsicle sticks licked clean. Past the bar-beque station, I find the pond where many geese swim. A scent cascades from its shores. Goose poop! There is so much of it! I sniff. I sniff deeper, snorting wildly, and test the ground with my paw. It's soft, rich with scent—the best kind of dirt.

My fur stands on end.

Suddenly some instinct kicks in, and I'm digging, then I'm *really* digging, dark clouds all around me. The air is thick with the smell of birds.

A few geese flock toward me, trying to stop my progress. They honk and flap their awful wings. I ignore them, dirt on my face, my whiskers, my eyelashes; it stains my fur and blackens my tongue. Eventually, I pause, staring down at the hole and piles of dirt by my paws. What have I done? It all happened so fast.

I look behind me.

No one in my family has noticed the dirt, the ruin, but they will. I'm not allowed to dig large holes. So I make a fast decision and eat the evidence, although I swore off dirt many moons ago. It is so dry in my mouth. I lap up pond water, continue, and then take a step back, flustered but satisfied with my work.

Back at the gazebo, the party goes on as planned. Someone drops off a large vanilla cake, as well as birthday hats in the shape of cones. Guests arrive. No one seems to like the hats but we wear them anyway, the elastic straps tight under our chins. People clap. Around Emmaline is a halo of balloons. She stands on the bench of a picnic table, bopping side to side in her summer dress. Below her, Max lights all six candles on the cake. Mom and Dad smile but only with their teeth.

Everyone sings.

"You've gotta make a wish," Uncle Reggie says.

So Emmaline makes a wish. She closes her eyes tightly and blows out the candles, and I lick the frosted ends as she pulls them out: vanilla is my favorite, and hers, too. After the cake, she skips down to the pond with her friends and tosses party chips to the geese. Next they whoosh down the slide over and over, their hands in the air. It's around then—as the sky turns a darker blue—that I notice the roiling in my belly.

All that dirt, it churns.

We unwrap presents. We play pin the tail on the donkey. Max feeds me a small slice of cake, and I eat only half. "What's the matter?" he asks. "You never say no to cake." His eyebrows press together, concerned. *But I'm fine,* I tell him, *just fine*—and to prove it, I grab some wrapping paper and thrash it around.

Back in the minivan, Uncle Reggie asks Emmaline, "So, what'd you wish for?"

She throws her arms into the air. "Wishes are *secret*!"

"Ah," he says, chuckling, "I forgot."

"But I could've wished for a pony."

My stomach tosses. It twists and turns.

Max asks, "Did you?"

And Emmaline says, "Nope!"

Dad pipes in from the front seat: "Well, Cosmo would like to be pony-size, I think. If we fed him as much as he wanted, then —"

I can no longer hold what's in my stomach. I blow. The van nearly swerves off the road.

"What the—?" Dad says.

"Oh my goodness," Mom says.

And Emmaline just starts screaming, because the damage is extensive. Dirt and pond water should not be consumed, especially in large quantities. The contents of my stomach clings to the seats, the floor. Everyone rolls down the windows, and we pull over at the first gas station—Mom rushing in to grab paper towels and whatever cleaning products she can find. I'm sulking, my tail so firmly between my legs that it cannot go any farther.

"You okay, Cosmo?" Max keeps asking me. "What did you eat?"

Outside, Dad's yelling at Mom, "Well, he obviously got into something!"

And Mom's yelling back, "*You* were supposed to be watching him! Do I have to do absolutely everything?"

Uncle Reggie leads me out of the car and washes my bib with a water bottle and some paper napkins. "You're gonna be just fine," he says. "I'll tell you one thing, you sure know how to give a performance." He's trying to be kind. But my tail still tucks, because this—this, too—is my fault.

That night, after the car is cleaned and after I'm washed with rosemary soap, Emmaline plops down next to me on the porch. Max has gone inside for some cheese crackers, and I'm waiting patiently. She lifts up one of my ears, so she can see inside it. "I'll tell you my wish," she says, angry voices in the background.

But I think I already know it.

Soon, it begins to feel like summer every day.
Humans play fetch with hard balls on TV. The
weather turns clammy and hot. I find myself gravi-
tating toward the air conditioner in Max's bedroom.
After dance practice, as we invent stories about what
the movie set will be like—with food carts and folding
chairs and stars all around—we lounge beneath the
cool streams of air, our jowls vibrating with the draft.
Nights are even worse, alternating between too hot
and too cold. I try to keep my panting to a minimum
so Max can sleep.

"Cosmo," he grumbles. "You sound like a train."

Some evenings, I crawl into bed with him, his arms

floating over me. It's a safe feeling—so wonderful that I never move away, even when the heat of it becomes almost too much to bear. I guess I want the security. Because the truth is, while the season is changing, our lives are changing more.

"Do we have a chance?" Max asks suddenly, one morning at the dance club.

"At winning the competition?" Uncle Reggie says.

"Yeah."

Uncle Reggie pauses, tilts his head back and forth. "Well, Cosmo's got all the moves down, minus the showstopper. And he *does* have personality. So . . . we definitely have a chance of making an impression. That's no small thing."

But as Mom and Dad continue to fight, it *seems* small. An impression—an impression alone—won't get us the walk-on movie role. It won't save us from separation.

On the weekends, when we're not dancing, Max has begun mowing our neighbors' lawns.

Mom says, "He's too young to operate heavy machinery."

Dad says back, "Oh, it'll be good for him. Builds character."

I have a sneaking suspicion that the lawn mowing

is not just for money to buy the rocket supplies that Max wants. I think he's trying to get out of the house any way he can. He's retreating more and more into himself, and even speaks with Oliver less at the dance club.

There is a big barbeque on the Fourth of July, when the boom of fireworks erupts overhead, and several people toss me hot dogs. I do not catch them. Eye-mouth coordination has never been a talent of mine—and with my vision, it definitely isn't now. When I play fetch, I ensure that the ball or stick has dropped fully to the ground before I scoop it up. Otherwise, I run the risk of tremendous embarrassment: grasping with my jaw wide open, clamping down, and finding nothing but air.

Max and I practice a few of our moves for the neighbors—the middle of our routine, when I bow over and over, flicking my tail. By now, with a month and a half to the competition, we're polishing our choreography, but my confidence isn't particularly high. I wish our routine was smoother than it is. Fancier than it is.

And the sheepdog! The sheepdog is gaining ground. At the club, it dances in the corner with perfect steps, flipping its ears so its fur shivers. It looks striking. So does Elvis, with his sleek black coat and deep, graceful

bowing. Even Noodles has honed her head toss. I, on the other hand, can't seem to master our big move — no matter how much we practice, no matter how much I hide the pain in my paw, which is worse than ever, a sharp sting, impossible to ignore. But I'm trying; I'm trying the best that I can.

Mid-July, Max starts bringing Emmaline to swim lessons at the local pool. She spends most days in those inflatable armbands. They are great fun to poke with your nose but do not squeak like Mr. Oinkers. I wish I could be there with her at the lessons. In fact, I have offered to go, waiting patiently by the front door. However, I am told to *stay,* the worst command in the history of commands, and am left to imagine it: Emmaline probably paddles like I do, with just her nose, eyes, and ears above the water.

In the evenings, I consciously try to slow things down. Summers always fly, fly, fly until they are gone. So I cherish everything about those summer nights, which Danny and Sandy also note in *Grease.* Nights can be slow. They can be Max, Uncle Reggie, and me on the porch, the satisfying crunch of potato chips in our mouths. They can be the three of us watching the rain, the big thunderstorms rolling in from the coast. Everything hums. The world is wet and warm.

"You excited for the competition?" Uncle Reggie asks Max one night. We are eating macaroni and cheese from small bowls.

Max just shrugs. "I'm just not sure what the judges and the casting director are looking for. If we're good enough for them — for the movie."

"Don't worry about the prize," Uncle Reggie says with a wave of his hand. "I mean, it would be cool. But what matters is having fun, right? Breaking you out of your shell?"

Max barely forms a word. "Mmm."

"What is it?" Uncle Reggie asks.

And Max says, "Nothing. It's nothing."

Sometimes, he is so hopelessly human — refusing to say exactly what he means.

That same night, he falls asleep early, one hand tucked underneath his cheek. I am still on guard, forever watchful. The sliding door remains shut after the raccoon incident, but I worry that the sheepdog could infiltrate the house through other means. Jumping through the window screens? Ringing the doorbell and simply walking in? All possibilities must be considered. I pin my ears back. And that is when I hear whispers in the kitchen.

I decide to investigate, identifying any weak spots

that the sheepdog may discover. My collar and tags jingle as I slink down the hallway. If Mom and Dad notice my approach, nothing in their body language suggests it. They are facing each other in the half dark, exchanging smells. Scents swirl between them.

Here is a little-known fact about me. In my youth, I would jump on people to greet them. Yes, I know. It's difficult to imagine now: me on my hind legs, launching myself into the open arms of family and friends. But I was so filled with love for them, and relief that they had appeared once more, that it literally could not be helped. Over the years, I broke the habit and adapted "the jump" into "the paw." The paw is still very effective. A swift paw to the knee says: *Hey, I am here. It is nice to see you. Please pet my head.*

At the edge of the kitchen, I feel my preferred paw (right, not left) lift slightly off the ground, but something tells me it just isn't the time.

Mom runs her hands through her curls. "We can't keep doing this. We can't keep pretending that everything's fine, that *this family* is fine . . ."

"So what are we supposed to do, then?" Dad asks, crossing his arms. Tension grips at his face.

"Don't ask me questions like that."

"Like what?"

"Questions you already know the answer to."

I'm still waiting for them to acknowledge my presence when my teeth start to chatter. Sometimes this happens when I'm cold, when a sharp breeze cuts through the thickness of my fur, but on very rare occasions, they chatter with worry.

"Oh, Cosmo," Mom says in a soft voice, her gaze finally turning in my direction. "Come here. It's okay."

I waver. On some level, I know that nothing *feels* okay, but I'm grateful for the attention. Slowly, I drop my head and pad toward her, pressing my muzzle into the clean fabric of her skirt.

"We'll figure it out," Dad says, whether to me or to Mom, I can only guess.

"The kids—"

"I know," he says. "I know."

For a moment it is like the early days, when it was just the three of us: Mom, Dad, and me. We are so close to one another. I want them to slip off their shoes. I want them to clasp each other's hands and dance. *Can't you see?* I tell them with a look. *Can't you see that this is breaking my heart?*

"I think we should go on a trip," Dad finally says.

"David . . ."

"No, hear me out. It would be good for us. To get

181

out as a family . . . Isn't your brother at the beach this week? We could join him. In a separate house, but he'll be there, and it could be nice." Dad brings his hand to his mouth. "Just say yes. Please."

I wait for her response, ears up. Through the chattering of my teeth, I hear her say: "All right."

The beach is my favorite place in the entire world.
I credit this to my earliest origins—I was born in a house not far from the shore—and also to my love of sand, which is not as chewy as it appears, but still adds a wonderful texture to burgers dropped on the ground. It was at Myrtle Beach that Max first invited me to swim. I remember stepping shyly into the ocean, the waves warm like bathwater, and feeling free in this remarkable new way.

"You can do it!" Max urged me on. "That's it, Cosmo! Swim!"

The water and I, we *danced*. There is no other way

to describe it. Paddling came so naturally, as if I was bred to do it.

Every summer after that, when the community pool opened, I found myself drawn to the water. I'd break free from my leash—followed by Mom's long shriek of "No, Cosmo, no!"—and charge with abundant energy toward the pool, leaping into the air and landing on the surface with a belly flop. I was always kicked out of the water shortly after that. As easy as it was to enter the pool, it was difficult to exit: I'd try to climb the small ladder, slip. Attempt to hoist myself onto the concrete, tumble. Most times, Dad would trudge into the deep end as I paddled around. "You darn dog," he'd say, a smile on his face, scooping me out with his strong arms.

Here is what I adore most about the ocean: no one says, *You are not allowed to be here.* The ocean is free territory. Fish swim there! And whales! Anyone can. Plus, every time I dip into the waves, Max is right beside me. He is a brilliant swimmer. Then again, he is a brilliant everything. I can only paddle forward with neat, tidy flicks of my paws—but him! You should see him go! He can backstroke. Dive. Splash the water with his beautifully flat palms. "I wish it could always be like this," he said to me once. We were

floating near the shore, letting the tide drift us in and out. I told him I wished for the same thing. That night, I dreamed of salt water, of catching fish in my mouth.

I hope this trip is like that—like old times. My heart cannot take it otherwise.

Mom and Dad announce our family vacation over breakfast, the morning after I discover them whispering in the kitchen. Neither of them is eating the food they've prepared.

"How would you two like to go to the beach this weekend?" Dad asks.

Max sits up straighter in his chair. "Really?"

"Really," Mom says. She smells tired.

Max says, "It's kind of close to the competition . . ."

I have the same worries, about losing momentum and risking our shot at the movie prize, but I also realize: I need the rest. *My paw* needs the rest. This will be good for us.

"Honey," Mom says, "you've practiced *so* much. And you'll still have some time when you get back."

Emmaline chews her pancakes, pushing them around in her mouth. "Do I have to wear my floaties?"

Max says, "You can come in the water with me, Em."

"*Without* my floaties?"

"Only if we stay really close to the shore."

185

Dad says, "It's a plan, Stan."

And so, days later, Max builds a nest out of old beach towels in the back of the minivan. I climb in next to him with the help of Dad, who lifts me from behind. "How much are we feeding you, Cosmo?" he says, struggling under my weight. Emmaline decides to snuggle up with Max and me, although there is plenty of room in the middle seats. On previous journeys, she has complained about the warmth and smell of my breath, as I pant through small towns and stretches of nothing but grass and power lines. I'm not sure what has changed.

Before we even leave the neighborhood, Emmaline pulls out her favorite book. It features a dinosaur named Harold. The human alphabet has always baffled me, no matter how long I focus on the letters. Luckily, the book has bright, beautiful pictures—and with the help of Max and Emmaline, who are both skilled in the art of human language, I've read the book several times. It is a complicated story. The crucial information is that Harold lives by the sea and likes to chew bubble gum. Sometimes, Dad does Harold's voice, which is upbeat and soothing. I find that I like it very much.

When we stop the minivan for an early lunch, Max

feeds me small pieces of beef burrito and gives me water from a bottle, and later Mom asks me through a cloud of gas: "Oh my gosh, Cosmo, what did you eat?" *Exactly what Max gave me,* I think. *What else?* We roll down the windows, and I stick my head out as Emmaline says, "Mommy, let's play I Spy."

"I spy," Mom says, "with my little eye, something that starts with *C.*"

"Car!" Emmaline says.

"Cosmo?" Max guesses.

I barely hear him over the rush of the air. But as we cruise down the highway, my ears flapping, I am struck with the overwhelming sense that this trip could be a fresh beginning for all of us. I don't know why. Something about the way the sun is beaming down. I can feel the lightness in our hearts. Maybe at the beach, Dad won't sleep on the couch. Maybe there will be no dishes breaking.

We drive on and on, into the new day.

The car stops in the driveway of a large house
surrounded by sweet-smelling trees. Max barely waits
for Dad to remove the keys before he hops out and
runs toward the hammock. Emmaline stretches her
legs. I do the same. Nothing feels quite as good as a
deep stretch after a long car journey, when your muscles are achy and tight.

Sufficiently limber, I plod up the porch steps. Mom
unlocks the door, and my nose leads me inside. Upon
the arrival of somewhere new, I take it as my duty to
sniff every square inch of the property, categorizing
scents as either "friendly" or "worrisome." Two spots
of carpet where a pair of dogs once lay? Friendly. A

popped balloon underneath the kitchen sink? Worrisome. A stray cat hair by the air vent? Undecided. Largely, I am convinced that the property is safe.

Dad begins setting up the wire kennel by the washing machine. I know that the kennel is only for traveling (it remains in the closet at home), but its presence still frustrates me. Humans assume—since dogs once lived in the darkness of caves—that kennels are no different. But humans were in the caves, too. Technically, Max, Mom, Dad, or Emmaline should climb inside the kennel *with* me.

In Emmaline's younger years, she did. She would pretend she was a dog, barking and panting and wagging her hindquarters. I wanted to explain to her that being a dog was more complex than that (she was oversimplifying the matter), but I never found the right moment. Besides, it was flattering. Not once did she pretend to be a giraffe, a turtle, or a cat.

Everyone unpacks for a few minutes. I set Mr. Oinkers in a place of prominence on the couch, so he may also adjust to his new surroundings. Max, apparently already tired of the hammock, runs in to claim the twin bed as his. He and Emmaline become like rubber balls, bouncing around the house.

"Save some of that for swimming," Mom says to

189

them, packing a beach bag. She grabs a water bowl for me, as I have learned never to drink salt water, ever, under any circumstance.

We gather the rest of our supplies—boogie boards, sunscreen, towels—and travel down a wooden bridge between several houses. It leads us directly to the ocean. *The ocean!* I had almost forgotten its scent. That undrinkable water! Seagulls! Once, I came very, very close to catching a seagull. Dad swears I was more than ten feet from the bird, but I know the truth; I flew that day. A dog has never jumped higher since.

It's the hottest part of the afternoon, so there are fewer people on the beach: older humans under striped umbrellas, their coolers wafting the scent of turkey sandwiches and something vaguely fishy. The five of us rush down to the wet sand, although I am slower because of my hips. Max sets up our beach towels far enough away from the dog poo area that only I can smell it. Once we're settled, I assume the position: back against the ground, belly exposed, legs halfway in the air. I wriggle around, marking the spot, until I feel the cool layer of wetness beneath me. Until the sand and I are one.

Later, as the waves trickle toward us, Max starts digging a moat with his bare hands. I am eager to

help, and work paw-over-paw at the loosely packed ground, sand flying all around us.

Emmaline giggles. *"Cosmooooo, you're making a mess."*

"He's helping," Max says.

I'm glad that someone understands.

Inside the moat, they build a sand house. It is magnificent. It is everything a sand house should be: tall and wide, with many holes for windows, and spirals that dart off in various places. "We should live here," Emmaline says, piling another wet handful on top of the structure, "with Mommy and Daddy and Cosmo."

I like our normal house better, but I don't say as much. I'm tremendously happy just to be here with them.

For the rest of the afternoon, we sunbathe. We eat apple slices and keep them away from the seagulls, which maintain their distance. (Perhaps their leader remembers who I am.) We watch Emmaline run back and forth into the shallowest water, plugging her nose with her fingers, the sea turning her curls flat and damp.

"Come on," Dad says, pulling Mom up by the hands. "Swim time."

Mom relents. "You know how I feel about seaweed on my legs."

191

"Mommy, *please,*" Emmaline says.

"Yeah, please?" Max says.

For a moment, I merely observe them. I stand at the edge of the water, letting the waves lick the tops of my paws. The four of them wade out on boogie boards, laughing and splashing in the water. I wish more than anything to freeze this moment. I bark, bark again—because we are so happy, and I can't think of a better way to tell them how much I love them, how I could watch them play all day long.

Max turns around and calls out to me. "What're you waiting for, silly dog?"

So I romp into the surf, feeling all the years wash away.

The next two days are nothing short of magical.
Uncle Reggie is staying at the other end of the beach,
and in the mornings he greets us with donuts, the
very sweet kind. Together we rent a small boat and
coast through the waterways, where I bark at many
fish. We swim. Oh, do we swim! My legs become so
tired from paddling. And in the afternoons, we hang
our beach towels on laundry lines and play hide-and-
seek behind them. "Where am I?" Max says. "Cosmo,
come find me!"

I do, every time. I would follow his voice anywhere.

The third evening, Uncle Reggie asks, "Anyone
want hot dogs?"

What a ridiculous question! Don't we all? Dad throws some on the grill, and Mom sets the glass table on the porch with napkins that flutter in the wind. I'm happy to see that there is no silverware; everyone is returning to nature. Max digs in first, eating with his hands. His fingers glisten with ketchup and mustard, which I lick, eventually consuming a hot dog of my own. Max cuts the meat into little pieces and scatters them across the deck. Apparently this is to keep me from gorging myself too quickly, but I enjoy the spirit of it, the hunt of it. I pounce on each piece. I chomp.

Max watches me, smiling. I realize with both concern and delight that I have not seen him smile so widely in many weeks. I miss his laugh, the way he folds his arms around his stomach and doubles over, his curls bouncing everywhere.

After dinner, Max guides me to my wire crate to spend some quality time with Mr. Oinkers, who is adjusting well. Max tells me about an island in the Bahamas run by wild pigs that wade in sparkling blue waters. Whether this is true or not, I find it comforting that Mr. Oinkers may be closer to his natural habitat.

Max locks the kennel door. "Sorry, Cosmo. I'd take you with us if I could."

He looks genuinely regretful.

It is not a secret that there are places in Myrtle Beach where dogs are not allowed. The town is full of them: restaurants that serve butter and crab, little shopping arcades, rickety amusement parks with strange rides that go up and swiftly down. On the way in, we passed a playground with plastic dinosaurs. Emmaline asked if one of them was Harold, the hero of her picture book. No one acted like this was a silly question. We all carefully considered it and determined that Harold was elsewhere.

Now Dad drapes a beach towel over the wire of my kennel, so everything becomes cool and dark. I listen to my family's steps—out of the house, onto the porch—as they leave to play miniature golf. Sometime later, I decide to sleep, so the hours will pass more quickly. What I do not anticipate is waking up to a slamming door.

And then, Max's voice.

"Even here!" he's yelling. "You guys just can't stop fighting! This was supposed to be *nice*. It was just putt-putt!"

I'm shocked. Max never yells.

"Honey," Mom says, "we didn't mean to—"

"Tell me the truth! You treat me like such a baby.

You think I don't see things or know things but I do! Even Emmaline can see it, and she still thinks that frogs can talk."

My mouth tastes funny, as it often does after sleep. I feel groggy and overwhelmed. What is happening? And what does it have to do with frogs?

"You're right," Mom says evenly. "You're completely right. Everything you're saying makes sense, and I promise you—I pinkie swear it—that we'll talk about it. I just want us to make the best of this while we can."

I wait for Max's response, but it doesn't come. Instead, he pulls the beach towel off my kennel and opens the door. I know instinctively to follow him: creaking my legs to a stand and curving into his bedroom, where he switches on the small TV and collapses into a heap on the floor.

I was not there tonight. Dogs do not play mini golf (although we would undoubtedly have the skill). So I have to piece together what happened. It takes me a while to work out the details, and I rely a lot on imagination. Perhaps someone stole the golf balls. An aggressive squirrel could have invaded the course. What I know for sure is that this is not the happy new beginning I predicted for us. I listen for Emmaline's

and Dad's voices—and I find them somewhere out-side, maybe on the porch. Uncle Reggie is gone. We are all in our separate spaces, our own worlds.

Max clicks the TV remote. And you would not believe what's on the Discovery Channel! A program about wolves—my ancestors!

"This okay?" Max says absentmindedly.

Very much so, I think to myself. It may be the only okay thing about tonight.

We watch for more than an hour. As it turns out, the human construction of a "wolf pack" is com-pletely wrong. Recently, scientists have discovered that wolves live in families, the way people do: with a mom, a dad, and their children. To which I say, *But of course!* If anyone had asked me, I could have hypothesized this much earlier. When Max was younger—and I was, too—we would play-wrestle in the grass, our backs muddy, our hearts full, until we were panting and tired. We grew up together. The word *owner* has never appealed to me, because Max and I, we are brothers.

At the end of the program, Dad comes into Max's bedroom, knocking on the open door. "Hey, kiddo."

"Hey," Max says, but does not look in his direction.

"How about some ice cream?"

"I'm not that hungry."

"You don't have to be *hungry* for ice cream." A pause. Another pause. "Well, if you change your mind, we have vanilla and mint chocolate chip." He hesitates in the doorway. For a second, I wonder if he will crouch down and watch TV with us, if everything will reverse itself, and suddenly we will remember that the beach is a place of happiness, no fighting allowed. But he sighs, turns, and leaves.

"You wouldn't do that," Max whispers to me when Dad is gone. I'm not sure what Max is referring to, yet I can sense the edge in his words. We curl up in a blanket, though it is very warm outside. Everything feels safer under a blanket.

"They don't treat me like a grown-up," Max says, a little louder. "I'm tired of all the pretending. They act like I don't know things. I just want them to treat me like I understand."

How do I tell him that I feel the same with most people? Sometimes I yearn so much to say, *Have I not eyes? Have I not ears?*

"I know you get it," Max says.

Yes.

"Sometimes I think you're the only one who does."

There's another knock on the door. Dad? It must be

Dad! Returning to say he'd like to watch TV with us, to curl up with us. But it's Mom who pokes her head in.

"Sweetie?" she says. Max stirs. "Can you join us in the other room, please? Family meeting." Then she looks at me very deliberately. "You, too, Cosmo. Come."

On instinct, my mind rolls over anything I could have possibly done wrong in the past days. Perhaps Mom discovered the empty cheese-cracker wrapper wedged underneath the minivan seat? Did Dad see the scratches on Max's new boogie board, as I clawed the edges in the surf?

Max follows me into the other room. My head is low. My tail is curved and sulky. I have never been able to hide my guilt—about anything. Some dogs? They can blissfully trot around, noses held high, while whole packages of stolen lunch meat rest comfortably in their bellies. But I am always the one shaking in the corner, lunch meat on my breath, my every movement shouting: *I did it! IT WAS ME!*

I feel the urge to pace as we enter the room. Straightaway, I can sense a dramatic shift in the air, like Max and I have walked directly into a thunderstorm and our paws are getting wet. Emmaline has folded herself into the corner of the couch, her arms wrapped around her knees. Dad is just the opposite.

He is in a chair that goes all the way back, except he is all the way forward, leaning toward us with his hands clasped. "Come on over here," he says gently to Max. "Come sit down." It does not escape my notice: this is Dad's "vet voice," the same cadence he uses alongside cold metal and cold tile, when he is trying to reassure me in the vet's office.

"What's going on?" Max asks, sliding slowly next to Emmaline. I scoot in by his feet, my head on his lap, trying to impart all the wisdom I can: *If he offers you a cookie, Max, don't be fooled!* I can't picture Max with a plastic cone wrapped around his head, bumping into walls and the sides of doors.

"Well," Mom says, taking a seat on the other chair. "You've probably noticed that Daddy and I have been fighting a lot, and . . . we're very tired of fighting. We don't want to fight anymore."

Dad sighs a long sigh. "Mommy and I love you so, so much. That hasn't changed. That will never change—do you understand? It's just, we don't feel the same way about each other that we once did, and—"

"And we want to do what's best for this family," Mom finishes, "for us and both of you."

Max's jaw clenches.

Emmaline pulls her knees tighter to her chest.

"We're getting a divorce," Dad says.

And there it is. There's the word, out loud, in the room. My teeth chatter, and I start to feel as if I've eaten too much dirt again, my stomach bloated and roiling.

"This is so messed up!" Max explodes, jumping to a stand. "You take us on this vacation and then you just . . . you just . . ." He's shaking. The whole room is shaking.

"You can be angry," Mom says quietly. "It's okay if you're angry."

And Dad says even quieter, "We tried. That's why we're here—we were still trying."

"Well, you didn't try hard enough," Max growls as Emmaline bursts into tears.

I understand his anger, because I don't fully comprehend the idea myself—that sometimes, if you are human, you can fall out of love.

Mom squishes the heels of her hands to her eyes. Dad runs his hands through his hair, over and over. Emmaline is slumping, and Max looks ready to flee.

It becomes real in those moments. All of it, real. The possibility of separation.

Us, apart.

"I know you probably have a lot of questions," Mom says.

And I do. Are Max, Emmaline, and I going to stay together? Will I go with Dad, and Max with Mom, like the boy at Max's school? We are inseparable. *Insepa-rable!* At least give us until the dance competition to prove it. Because Max and I, if we win that walk-on movie role, *can* prove it.

I start whimpering softly. Some occasions are too hard to bear.

"I want you to know," Dad says, clasping his hands, "it probably doesn't seem like it right now, but every-thing *will* turn out all right."

I have always trusted Mom and Dad. In all the time I can remember, there were only one or two instances when my food dish arrived late. But I detect some-thing different in their voices now. Something fragile and unsure.

Mom says, "Daddy is . . . Daddy is going to take some time away for a while. And when he comes back, we'll . . . decide about living arrangements. We don't know about any of that yet. There's . . . there's just too much to figure out. But everything's going to be all right, like Daddy says. I promise."

"Promise?" Max exclaims, standing up from the couch. "You *promise*? That doesn't mean anything anymore. I'm going back to bed."

Dad moves to say something, but Mom cuts him off with "David, let him go."

Max darts away, and I follow.

Back in his room, I pace. I try to ease the tension by pressing Mr. Oinkers's belly with my snout, until he produces his trademark noise. Beside myself, desperate to offer comfort, I shove Mr. Oinkers into Max's lap, hoping that this gesture will express everything I feel. *My toy is yours, Max. My heart is yours.* The pig stares up at us with his black threaded eyes, and I wonder if it'll be enough.

"Thanks, boy," Max says after a moment, accepting the gift. He pets the top of Mr. Oinkers's head and sniffles. "You really want me to have him?"

Yes.

"You know I can't take him from you."

Please.

"But we can share him, okay?"

The love I feel for Max swells, and I wish—more than anything—that I could answer him in a way that he could fully understand. Just then, Emmaline knocks on the door and slips inside Max's room. The three of us hold each other for a very long time on the floor. We cry. We curl up on the bed together.

And we gaze at the stars out the window.

"The universe is so big," Max once said, "bigger than you could ever imagine." I think about that now. I think about how we've spent so long trying to avoid this moment. But you can never outrun the inevitable—even if you are fast and young and do not have arthritis in your legs. Even if you have all the space in the universe to run.

Divorce is a sheepdog, waiting in a dark corner, picking at our weakest spots.

I must have fallen asleep, because the next thing I know, all the lights are off. The beach house is silent, Emmaline has returned to her room, and Max is softly shaking my shoulder. My nails have been recently trimmed, so they make little sound as I rise and follow him. From what I gather, it is the middle of the night. The glass door shows me an enormous moon. Max must be hungry. Why else would he be awake now? Maybe his stomach was rumbling. That's it. We're traveling to the kitchen for a midnight snack.

I try to cling to this assumption, even when Max grabs his sneakers and clips on my leash. Should

I bark? Alert Mom and Dad of the situation? Or is Max planning on leaving the house so I may relieve myself? Did I somehow give him the wrong impression? I feel paralyzed with indecision. I'd hate to get Max in trouble, but leaving the house at night is both risky and forbidden.

Max!

He slips out the door quickly, before I can properly assemble my thoughts into actions. Panicking, I follow in his footsteps. If Max wants to travel into the night, I must be there to protect him.

Outside, streetlamps glow. The waves are louder than anything else I can hear. I expect Max to explain himself. In fact, I *beg* him to explain himself: whimpering, shoving my wet nose against his hands. His skin is bitter with sunscreen.

"I know," he says to me. "I'm sorry. But after everything that just happened, I couldn't sleep and I couldn't breathe in there. Don't worry: I left a note for Emmaline."

This triggers something in my memory — our conversation when it snowed, about running away. I thought that was hypothetical! Is that what we're doing right now? Are we running away? Guilt roils through my belly.

I forgot Mr. Oinkers.

I just left him in Max's room. What happens if he wakes up to discover I've abandoned him? And what about snacks? How can we survive without snacks? I may boast about my hunting skills, but I never imagined I'd have to *use* them! Can you imagine me, subsisting on pinecones and small creatures?

Wait . . . Max wouldn't run away without a backpack!

Max doesn't have a backpack. He wouldn't leave his signed astronaut photograph or his moon rocks. But when I look up again, I notice it: a small bag, slung over his shoulder. And this terrifies me, as we cross the bridge between houses, as the ocean opens up before us. The beach is empty. I have never seen it empty. And the stars! The sky is brighter than back home. In our neighborhood, you are lucky to see a few constellations, with all the houses and the streetlights. But here, the stars are so abundant and so close that I can almost smell them.

"I couldn't let them separate us," Max whispers to the night, "now that it's actually happening."

Panic spikes in my chest. We should be inside. We should be safe in the house. But Max doesn't say another word, and we walk and walk, prints in the sand, until my left paw begins to tire. It's sore, the jabs of pain returning. I wonder if I limp, if he *sees* me limping, then we can turn back. Maybe no one will notice that we've left.

Suddenly, he's turning up a side street, away from the beach, and the pavement is warm underfoot. "It shouldn't be too far," he says, his voice almost a whisper. "I saw it when we were coming in. A few blocks, I think."

Normally I would love this—just the two of us, exploring the night. If we were in the backyard, we would be catching fireflies and maybe there'd be snacks. Max might be pointing out the constellations, and I'd burrow my snout in the scruff of his neck until he said, "Cosmo, your nose is so *cold*." Then I'd settle down for a belly rub, maybe a snooze in the grass, and he'd wake me when it's time to return inside. He always rouses me so softly, raising my paw up and down.

As I've said, Max is incredibly smart. But I know how emotions can override brilliance, how bad thoughts can sneak in and tackle good ones. I, too, have fallen victim to this; my judgment is not always sound. Yet right now, I can see very clearly: if we keep on this path, we're heading for trouble. So I bark. I

bark as loud as my lungs allow, the noise feral and deep from my belly. It echoes down the tiny street, bouncing off parked cars and garbage cans.

Three paces ahead, Max spins around with his finger to his lips. "Cosmo, *shhh.*"

He's never shushed me before, and I hate the feeling; it's like a sharp poke in the ribs. I shrink back, my tail between my legs, a low whimper escaping me. Immediately, something changes in his expression.

"Oh, Cosmo," he says, voice quivering. "I'm sorry. I didn't mean it." Then, just as quickly, he throws his head back with a "No! No, no, *no.* I forgot *water.* For you and me. It's a long bus ride."

He tugs lightly on my leash, urging me to follow, but my head is throbbing with all his words. Bus ride?

"I think there's a gas station right by the station," he says. "I'll just . . . Yeah, I'll just get some there. I'm so, so sorry, boy. I can grab us some crackers, too. The cheese ones. The ones you like."

For a moment, this distracts me, because I do love those crackers. Tang and salt, smoothness and crunch. One time I had them with additional spray cheese, which comes neatly packed in a can, and tastes incredibly strong, and—

No!

I'm ashamed to find my mouth watering. How can I think about food at a time like this? How can I think about *my bladder* at a time like this? Even as I walk, it presses against the edges of me. Max knows that when I'm stressed, I need to relieve myself as soon as possible, and sometimes I cannot hold it, no matter how hard I try.

A car slows and then passes us. Somewhere in the distance, a seagull caws. And I feel myself dragging farther and farther behind, my leash extending to its fullest.

After what seems like hours, we arrive at a gas station. The sliding doors whoosh open, and the coolness travels outside. My nose twitches, stings: the air smells of chemicals.

"You!" a man shouts from across the store. "No dogs. See the sign?"

I cannot read, I say, feeling offended.

Max sucks in a breath. "Cosmo, can you wait right here, please? Can you stay?" He quickly loops my leash to a bike rack, moonlight flickering all around us. "I'll just be two seconds. Two seconds, I promise." And I make a promise, too—not to take my eyes off him, to watch him doggedly. Yet he disappears into the aisles, the cheap food packages swallowing him up. I

tug at the leash, straining to see him. I imagine that my paw does not hurt, that my legs do not ache, and I throw my whole body weight into it.

Nothing.

Standing there, panting on the sidewalk, the quivering yellow lights washing me with glow, the enormity of the situation sinks in—*really* sinks in. Max and I, we are *running away*. We are leaving Emmaline and Mr. Oinkers and the squirrel bushes in our backyard. We are leaving our neighborhood, the dance club, Uncle Reggie, and Mom and Dad. My biggest fear is separating from Max—but this isn't right. This isn't right, and I know it.

Thumbs! If only I had thumbs! To untie this leash so I *can* separate myself from Max—for the greater good, for both of us. If I disappear, maybe he'll look for me. Maybe we won't get on the bus after all.

Then it comes to me, like a whisper on the breeze. *I have the soul of a dancer.* And I can use that—my newfound skills, my limberness—to twist out of this contraption. I spin. I tuck, bow, roll. And the leash unties, dropping free with a gentle thump.

Gaze darting around, I spot a hedge strewn with soda cans, not too far away. I don't know where I find the strength, but I begin limping across the parking lot. I can make it, hide there, and Max will have to find me.

Two large buses pull into the gas station, their stench polluting the night, and I must be faster.

"Cosmo?" Max's voice. Max's voice behind me. "Oh, no. Cosmo! Here, boy! Cosmo!"

But I won't turn around. I won't. With all the energy I have left, I let out a howl and —

Suddenly. It's so sudden.

The shriek of tires. The scream from Max's lungs. The headlights of a car, coming straight for me.

He bought the cheese crackers, the ones I like.
They're in a small plastic bag with a bottle of water
for us to share. I watch them slip from his hands as he
rushes after me yelling, "Cosmo, *no!*"

There are brakes slamming and car tires skidding—too much noise. According to the Turner Classic
Movies channel, in moments like this, your whole life
is supposed to flash before your eyes. What I think
of is Max and Emmaline and how unfair I've been to
turtles. Crossing roads is tricky after all.

Then Max's hands are pushing against me. And
we're tumbling—rolling to the side as the car nar-
rowly misses us, as it swerves off into the bushes at

the last possible second. I know I'm old. I know that most humans would not believe it a great tragedy for me to be struck by a vehicle in a gas station parking lot, after all the wonderful years I've lived. In the grand scale of things, my family and I are small: a speck in an ever-expanding universe. But I'm happy I survive. I have so much more to give.

And Max!

Did he . . . he just . . . ?

I'm splayed on the ground, and he's kneeling over me, shaking. He presses his forehead to my belly. "You were almost . . . You almost . . . And it would've been all my fault." He's crying before I can realize what's happening, before I can fully process just how lucky I am. My boy *saved* me. My boy jumped in front of *a car* for me. It strikes me all at once: how I've always assumed that I loved Max more than he loved me. But now I know the truth. It goes both ways.

Quick as the car came, the driver backs out of the bushes, skidding away. I can just about see the fuzzy dice hanging from his rearview mirror, black and white, puffy like the sheepdog. Max and I are left there, beneath all those stars. We look at each other then. For once, I don't wish I could form human words, because in those moments we say everything that needs to be said.

"You're right," Max whispers. "We shouldn't be running away, not like this."

He helps me to the sidewalk — and we wait until I gather my strength. When I stand again on shaky legs, he says, "I promise it's not far." He leads me across one street, turns down another wooden path, and trudges up to a house with a hammock and surfboard. There are blue flowers in the pots and shoes on the mat. Who lives here? And should we be knocking on the door in the middle of the night?

"We're safe here," Max says.

A breeze drifts from the coast, carrying lightning that splits the sky into little fragments. Everything glows.

Max knocks on the front door. Knocks again.

And Uncle Reggie answers.

"Max?" he says, rubbing his eyes. He peers around the corner, his head like a bird's. "What time is it? Where are your—?"

"They're getting divorced," Max blurts out. "They're getting divorced, and I didn't want to be separated from Cosmo, so I took him and we were going to run away, I even went to the bus station, but I didn't pack any water or cheese crackers, and Cosmo really likes this certain kind, and then he almost got hit by a car, and it would've been my fault—all my fault. I almost got him *killed,* Uncle Reggie, and I realized that the running away thing was so stupid, and I thought, well, I thought that you were here, we saw your house on the way in, and —"

Uncle Reggie steps forward and wraps his arms around Max. "It's okay," he says. "It's okay. You're here now . . . You're not injured, are you?"

Max shakes his head.

"You sure?" Uncle Reggie says.

"I'm sure."

"Cosmo's okay, too?"

"No thanks to me," Max whispers, which I don't completely understand—because he saved my life. For a long moment after that, no one moves. Then Uncle Reggie releases him, beckoning us to the back deck. It overlooks a marsh, moonlight trickling along the tall grasses. More and more lightning crackles through the sky.

"Storm's coming," Uncle Reggie says, shoving his hands into his pockets. "I hate to say this, but you know I have to call your parents, right? If they wake up and you're not there, they'll be scared to death."

Max sinks into a beach chair, wrapping a worn-out towel around his shoulders. Guilt wafts from him—and

he seems so, so tired, his head tipping back. "But do I have to leave? Can't Cosmo and I stay with you?"

Uncle Reggie nods somberly. "I'll see what I can do." He disappears inside as the rain starts—a light trickle that we endure. Max stretches out his hands and catches the droplets. He sticks out his tongue, his dark hair frizzing. When Uncle Reggie returns, there's a box of donuts in his hands. "Leftovers," he says. "Times like this, donuts help in a way that only donuts can. That's what my platoon leader used to say. Eat."

So we eat, Max breaking off stale pieces and feeding me from the palm of his hand.

"I spoke to your mom," Uncle Reggie says. "And she says you can stay till morning, if you want—if you promise never to do *anything* like this again." He sinks into the nearest chair. "Your parents are good people. Really good people, Max. I don't know all the details of it, but I know that they never meant to hurt you or Emmaline. That's the last thing they want."

"We didn't even . . ." Max says, his voice failing as lightning strikes in the distance. "We didn't even make it until the dance competition. They were supposed to see us, before any of this happened. We were supposed to *win,* and they were going to see us in that movie."

Uncle Reggie doesn't fully understand what Max means—not like I do. But still, he leans forward after a moment, clasping his hands. "Who's to say they still can't? And you got to spend time with Cosmo. You got to hang out with your *best friend.* Do you understand how special that is? I'd give just about anything to spend another day—just one more—with my dog, Rosie. We've been through so much together. Honestly, I thank God every day that you met me at the airport, because when I stepped off that plane without her, I felt like I was about to burst apart."

At this, Max's eyes begin to stream again—and I try to crawl into his lap, heavy as I am, tired as I am. I wiggle and squirm, setting my head on his shoulder, the chair creaking beneath our weight. He finishes another bite of his donut but leaves the rest. I can tell he isn't very hungry, and neither am I. Half of my piece rests on the porch.

"I'm sorry," Max finally whispers. "I'm sorry about Rosie. I feel the same way about Cosmo, which is why . . . I can't do the dance competition anymore."

Uncle Reggie's back straightens.

There are tears on Max's cheeks, in the corners of his mouth. "We've spent all this time . . . To show that we shouldn't be separated . . . And *I* almost separated

us, permanently. That was me. Cosmo almost *died*. And I just can't . . . I don't want to risk anything, or go anywhere, or trust myself to have good ideas. *I* was the one who wanted to do this competition, not Cosmo. He got dragged along."

That's not true! I tell him, shivering in the chair. I have always wanted to dance.

"Cosmo has loads of fun when he's out there," Uncle Reggie says. "And tonight was an accident. You love that dog. I'm not really sure where you're coming from, bud. What do you mean, 'to show that we shouldn't be separated'?"

It's like Max has mud in his ears. He treads on, distracted, his words cracking more and more. "I know I'm not making any sense, but it's how I'm feeling. I can't . . . I can't trust myself not to get him hurt. At least if he's with Dad, I'll see him again. I just can't, with any of this."

Uncle Reggie chews on his cheek. "You're old enough to make your own decisions. But I hope you change your mind."

"I won't," Max tells us, and that's the last thing he says all night.

The next morning, Max eats his cereal in silence.
We return to the beach house, where Mom hugs him,
and then Dad hugs him. He packs his suitcase in
silence. As the tide rolls in, Dad locks up the beach
house and drops the keys in the mailbox. The five of us
travel down near-empty roads and watch the sun shift
over the tops of houses. Halfway back, Max tucks his
forehead into the folds of my neck and keeps it there.

This time, we do not stop for beef burritos. I do not
stick my head out the window. My ears and jowls do
not flap in the glorious, glorious breeze. We simply get
in the minivan and emerge four hours later, stopping
only once for a potty break.

At home, beach towels and boogie boards are lifted from the trunk. Suitcases are emptied. Snacks are returned to cabinets. And Max crawls almost immediately into bed, along with Emmaline. I try to follow them, edging my nose under the covers, nudging Max's cheek with my snout. I bark once, but he doesn't seem to hear me. He pulls the sheets all the way over his head, so I turn circle after circle on the spot, anxious and attempting to lie down. I can't. Now more than ever, we should be practicing our choreography. We should be dancing! Because we might still have enough time—to nail the showstopper, win the competition, secure the movie role.

We can stay together, if we try.

That night, the hours come and go. Thoughts sift in and out like beach water, my eyes half-closed. Much later, I hear a noise in the living room and decide to stretch my legs. I find Dad sitting on the edge of the couch. He is staring into the distance, as I do when I'm thinking deep, deep thoughts. Then his shoulders begin to shake, and I hear him crying, too. It's a very quiet cry. My instinct is to run to him, to nudge my snout into his waiting palms, but instead I pause by the night-light. Most days I believe that I understand humans. I understand why they hate and why they love. But some days, I discover something new—a hidden complexity. And it startles me to my core.

This startles me.

It startles me how easily things can fall apart.

Back in bed, I sleep fitfully. Whenever I roll over, Mr. Oinkers lets out a wild squeak, and I cannot seem to get myself comfortable, no matter how many times I stand up, circle, and lie down again. Max and Emmaline barely drift off. They sigh a lot, like me, their bellies filling with air. When the sun finally comes up, we are bleary-eyed and exhausted.

I poke my nose outside Max's room, expecting to smell the same scents from last night: confusion and anger. But there is only soft lavender soap that Mom uses on her hands, and the faint aroma of yesterday's sandwiches. At first I think that no one besides Max, Emmaline, and me are awake, though I soon hear feet shuffling. It's Dad, in his room. When I tiptoe inside, Mom is not there—but a suitcase lays open on the bed.

"Hey, boy," Dad says, noticing my presence.

It crosses my mind that perhaps I should hide his shoe. Or both shoes? Yes, *both* shoes! He cannot leave without his shoes! The idea takes complete hold of me, and I begin to rush around frantically—from corner

to corner—searching for anything that even *smells* like a shoe.

"Whoa," Dad says. "Easy, boy. Easy."

But I'm scrambling.

Some part of me knows that Dad will leave, with or without his shoes, with or without his socks, with or without his ties. Yet what else can I do?

One of Dad's hands gently grabs me by the collar. The other touches my head in the soft way I like. Then he presses his forehead to mine and whispers, "I am so sorry, Cosmo. I am just so, so sorry." The warm scent of him washes over me. I lick his wrists, his hands, to tell him, *It is all right,* although it isn't. He needs comfort. My main responsibility is to Max—but I can see pain when it's happening right in front of me.

He lets go. At a loss, I jam my snout into a pile of his socks on the bed and snort in short, sharp bursts. Dad starts shoveling clothes into the suitcase as I glance up at him.

"Don't look at me like that, Cosmo," he says, wiping his nose. "I know this is . . . Eventually it'll be for the best." He moves the last pair of socks from beyond my reach. "Now, you be a good dog."

I take issue with this command. I *am* a good dog, always.

The suitcase clicks shut. Every floorboard seems to creak as he walks away. I follow him slowly outside, to the edge of the driveway, where Mom, Max, and Emmaline are waiting. There is a long silence before Dad tells Emmaline and Max: "I'm just going to Grandma and Grandpa's for a little while. I'll see you both real soon." He kisses their heads. "I love you. Remember that I love you so much."

Whimpering, I press myself firmly against Max's legs. We watch Dad slide into his car. Max sets his hand on the crown of my head and rests it there. I can feel him shaking through my fur, so I lick his fingers, his palms. I lick and lick—hoping the sadness will melt off him.

"It's okay," he says, but I know it's Max—not me—who needs convincing.

I bark loudly. Dad sticks his head out the window and tells me, "Good boy. Now stay." I can sense the seriousness in his words. *Stay. Stay with them. Stay with them, when I will not.*

The car pulls out of the driveway and begins to curve into the dusky morning light. It passes the squirrel bushes and the crow trees. It kicks up dust and spews exhaust. And I think hard about the word *stay*. Shouldn't I have some choice in the matter?

Out of all the commands in my life, I have disobeyed few. I made a decision when I was very young to be a *good dog* in every sense of the phrase. But I also promised to protect Max, doggedly, for the rest of my life. Surely one outweighs the other? So I spring forward. I trot. Then run, even though it hurts. I run after the car, now a blip on the horizon.

I run as fast as I can, until I can't run anymore.

Swans are terrible birds. They do not sit in trees, or let you chase them at picnics. I have heard rumors that they bite, that they stalk dogs of all breeds by public lakes. But one thing I know for certain is that swans stay together for life—penguins, too. The Discovery Channel covered this extensively. I didn't fully comprehend the importance of it then: how when one bond breaks, everything else breaks with it.

I listened for Dad's car for a long while after that, but he never did turn back around. For the next three nights, I wait. There is a special spot by the window where I poke my nose through the slit in the blinds. I watch for his headlights in the dark and listen for the mechanical *vroom* as his car pulls into the driveway. I picture myself barking triumphantly and then racing toward him across the lawn, rolling immediately onto my back. *Pet my belly,* I will tell him, *and all is well.*

As much as Max denies it, I think he harbors similar daydreams. He has such an expressive face; sometimes I can just see it. He will be doing the dishes and suddenly look up, his head stilling like mine when I am watching a bee in the yard. Then he will blink, shake his whole head, and go back to soaping the sponge.

He can talk to me, about anything, and I will listen. Instead we watch TV together as the sadness infects everything. It is there in the swaying of the grass and the whispers of the trees, in the clouds that gather in clumps, in the cereal that we eat and the air that we breathe. On my own, I am still rehearsing our choreography; I am still hoping that Max will change his mind—that we will take the competition stage, our moves undeniable and flawless. Because every moment, I'm waiting for it to happen. A phone call. A knock on Max's bedroom door. Something to signal that I'm leaving and Max is staying, that we are being split apart.

On the fourth night, I dream of Mom and Dad, dancing. They are in the kitchen, barefoot like they were when I was young. Mom is a vision in blue. Dad lifts his arm, as I have been taught to do with my front leg, and spins her. They smile at each other. And that is the whole dream. I wish there were more.

At least twice a day, I hear Mom speaking into the phone.

"I'm not sure if we're selling the house," she says one evening, her mouth pressed to the plastic. "No, we haven't—well, we've *discussed* it. Lawyers? I don't know. I just don't know."

To add insult to injury, Mom captures Mr. Oinkers, whom I've hidden underneath Max's bed. "Ah, there you are," she says to him. I bark as he is tossed unceremoniously in the wash. He spins. My head spins with him. And in the end, he smells so unbearably clean. I know Mom believes she's doing me a favor.

But in the wee hours of the night, I lick Mr. Oinkers until my tongue feels funny, desperate for his rich scent to return. *Something* must stay the same in all this chaos. You might say that I become obsessed. My ears pin back. My eyes narrow. On the floor of the living room, I nose-dive into him, over and over. The squeal in his tummy turns into nothing more than a

murmur. I am glad that no one was awake to witness this, because I am trying very hard to be strong. When I finally fall asleep, I have the strangest impression that the sheepdog is there, standing over me, its jowls drooping underneath all that fur.

With Dad gone, the chores stack up. Uncle Reggie helps where he can. And I do, too: after dinner, I wash the plates with my tongue, and when the grass grows long, I snip at bits with my teeth, swallowing too often, and eventually vomiting a bright green mound on the living-room carpet. Which I helpfully clean up as well. All in all, I find myself repeating: *We are fine. We are fine.* I wonder if I am now doing the thing that humans do, because none of us are fine at all.

The next week brings the biggest heat wave of the summer. Max drops ice cubes in my water bowl and spends more time with Emmaline than usual. They play on the swings in the backyard, although Max claims he is too old for swings. They swim at the neighborhood pool and return home with sunburned skin. When a heat wave practically knocks us out, they settle inside Emmaline's room. I find that her stuffed animals are tossed all over the floor. Emmaline's animals are off-limits; I learned that early in life. But I still nudge them gently back in line, as she had them before, to try and restore a sense of order in the household.

"Cosmo," Emmaline says later, "you drooled on all my animals."

You're welcome, Emmaline. You are very welcome.

Out of the corner of my eye, I notice that she has a stuffed pig as well. Should I bring Mr. Oinkers in to play? He often misses out on the fellowship of his own kind.

Emmaline stares at the tips of her dinosaur sandals, and then tilts her head at Max. "Do you think that when we grow up we'll be sad all the time?"

Max rears a stuffed horse onto its back legs and neighs, a startling noise coming from him. "I don't think all grown-ups are like that."

"My friend Sarah said that Daddy isn't ever coming back."

"Tell Sarah she's being mean."

They pause. The horse advances.

"Sarah's daddy never came back," Emmaline says. Max doesn't respond. "Will Daddy ever live with us again?"

"I don't know, Em."

Emmaline thinks very hard about this, her little eyebrows scrunched. Eventually, Max dips into the kitchen to prepare a snack—potato chips, by the smell of it. I can feel the resistance as Emmaline drags her fingers through my fur, her hands sticky with syrup from breakfast. "Cosmo," she says softly. "You still love me, right? You won't ever stop?"

I used to think that movies were perfect simulations of real life. The good guys beat the bad guys. Wars end. People fall apart like Danny and Sandy and then fall back together. But I'm starting to realize that we are all just doing the best we can.

That night in Emmaline's room, we flip through *Calvin and Hobbes,* a complex story about a boy and his pet tiger. When we come to a scene where Calvin discusses heaven, I find that his ideas are different from mine. I believe that the afterlife is a bright and endless sky. I believe that souls stay together: humans and dogs, humans and tigers, as it has always been.

"That was a sad one," Emmaline says quietly. "I liked it better when they ate tuna fish sandwiches."

"And pretended to be in space," Max agrees, tucking her into bed. I would help if I had opposable thumbs.

"Tell me another story?" Emmaline asks Max.

"You want me to read *Harold*?"

She shakes her head against the pillow. "You make one up."

Max says, "I don't know if I know how to . . ."

"Try," Emmaline says, tugging the sheets farther up her neck. "Please."

"Um . . . okay. Let's see . . . There once was a dog named Cosmo."

I raise my head higher, ears pricking.

"Like our Cosmo?" Emmaline asks.

Max nods. "Yeah, except he . . . saves the neighborhood. With a squirrel on his back. They fight crime together."

Well, this took a startling turn.

"They run through the woods," Max continues, hands darting out in front of him, "chasing away all the monsters."

"Is that it?" Emmaline says.

"Should there be more?"

"Yes! Cosmo needs to save the *whole world.*"

"I think he'd get hungry before that."

Emmaline smiles. "The squirrel has peanut butter."

They laugh about this, although I have notes on how to improve the story: Lose the squirrel. Keep the peanut butter. Max kisses Emmaline on her forehead, says good night, and goes to flick on the porch light.

He tells us it's for Dad, just in case he comes home.

I stay back for a moment, leaning against the bedsheets. Emmaline peers down at me in the near darkness. "I'll tell you a secret," she says, very seriously, lifting up my ear as she has always done. "I still want you to dance."

If I had a tongue that could fold over, that could form human words, I would have held Emmaline's glance and said, *I still want to dance, too.* Any day, Mom and Dad could tear us apart. So why not try and win the competition, as we planned? We might have time left. We might.

"Want to go on a trip?" Max says the next day, without the familiar lightness in his voice. He clips the leash on my collar, and I wheeze in the warm air.

It's deep summer—the kind of afternoon when the dark pavement is hot on my paws. I find myself aching to return to February, when snow fell so wonderfully from the sky. Popsicles are one of the only good things. Max has gotten into the habit, much to my pleasure, of sharing his with me. Whenever Mom witnesses this, she says, "You can't imagine where Cosmo's tongue has been." And yet I always can. It has licked jelly off the kitchen floor, and several minutes later cleaned my hindquarters. I see no problem with this.

Mom and Max are arguing frequently.

"Dogs' mouths are cleaner than humans'," he says.

"That's been scientifically disproven," she says.

We are at an impasse.

The four of us drive slowly through back neighborhoods, twisting and turning until we reach the grocery store. Max ties my leash to a rail and waits beside me on the curb, sipping lemonade from a box. He moves a water dish closer toward my snout. Droplets slosh everywhere.

"Make sure you're drinking enough," he says absentmindedly.

"I'll just be a minute!" Mom calls out behind us. She pauses at the entrance, pushing Emmaline in a cart—and she looks prepared to say something else. But then she disappears with Emmaline inside, where I am not allowed to follow.

I shake, a puff of loose fur clouding around me.

And I think. Part of me is startled by how normal everything is starting to feel: the grocery store, Mom buying Popsicles and kibble, the humid haze spreading across the parking lot. Three and a half weeks have passed since Dad drove away. There have been more phone calls. There have been forks and spoons tossed aggressively into the dishwasher. But we still eat. Mom still goes to yoga. Emmaline continues her swimming lessons. Day in, day out, everything is the same, and yet everything is different.

More and more, I hear Mom talking on the phone. Words like *moving* and *house* and *separation* ring through the air. Still, I dance. And I hope.

The sun beats down.

When I shake again, I see Uncle Reggie through my cloud of loose fur. He pops out of the store and pulls to a halt as he spots us.

"Cosmo!" he says.

I get a sudden thrill out of being noticed first. He stoops down to pet me, and I note the cheese wrapped in plastic, tucked in his bag. I do my best to appear like I'm fully invested in our interaction, and our interaction only.

Uncle Reggie gestures to a spot on the curb, right next to me. "Mind if I sit?"

"Go ahead," Max says.

He lowers himself down, elbows on his knees. "I called yesterday to see if you wanted to come over. How is everything?"

"It's . . ." Max says, but doesn't finish.

We wait in silence for a few moments, as people push grocery carts out to their cars. Birds fly over us, flapping their dark wings.

"It's hard to talk about this stuff," Uncle Reggie says. "I get that. Trust me, I do." He lets out a big sigh. "Did your mom ever tell you that I was just like you when I was a kid? I felt things, really strong."

Max tilts his head up. "How'd you stop?"

"Stop? Man, you don't want to stop. It's a blessing to feel. When you go numb, that's when the world really starts to shrivel up. You've got to channel it." Uncle Reggie places his hands on the sidewalk and leans back. I lick his fingers. "Think about it this way: a good dancer's supposed to feel with all their heart."

Max shakes his curls. "I . . . I can't go back there, though. To the dance club."

"Why not? Seriously, why not? When you were there, didn't you have fun?"

"Well, yeah. But that night at the gas station . . . I made a bad choice. And it would've been like half of me was missing, you know? If Cosmo got hit by that car?"

"But he didn't," Uncle Reggie points out.

"But it was *close,*" Max says, "and after that, it really just sunk in. The whole thing. How I almost lost him, how Mom and Dad were actually getting divorced. And I just wanted everything to *stop.* I wanted to stand still. I didn't trust myself to do anything but stand still."

"You were overwhelmed. People do irrational things when they're overwhelmed, like run off in the middle of the night. And quit dance competitions." He nudges Max. "I understand, though. It's not exactly the same, but I used to see something like it with a few soldiers in my platoon. They train for years, and then something happens—maybe they see a friend get injured in the line of duty, and that fear becomes paralyzing. Sometimes it's easier to freeze and try to feel nothing at all. Sometimes we can't help it. . . . But don't you miss it, Max? The club?"

"I . . . I guess I do."

"Do you guess?" Uncle Reggie asks gently. "Or do you know? Because in my experience, things like the dance club don't always come into our lives. Dogs like Cosmo don't always come into our lives. So when they do, it's our job—our *responsibility*—to view them as

gifts. I know that things haven't exactly turned out the way you planned, especially the night you tried to run away, but this dog loves you, and I love you, and your parents love you — and years from now, I don't want you to look back and think: I should have danced."

We wait.

I'm not sure what we're waiting for, until Max sighs. "I don't guess," he says, just as the sun starts to lower over the cars. "I don't *guess* I miss the dance club. I know."

"Then we should go."

"What about —"

"Don't worry about the unknown," Uncle Reggie says. "Do the competition to *face* the unknown. And do it for your friendship with Cosmo — because you're special together. You've both trained really hard, and you deserve this. Now, split-second decision. The club's meeting in fifteen minutes."

"But your groceries . . ."

"Forget the groceries. There are more important things than cheese."

Max can't help but laugh. Then he looks at me, his eyes searching mine. He takes a deep breath. "Do you think you can trust me, Cosmo?"

And, with a paw on his hand, I tell him: *Always.*

When Emmaline and Mom emerge, we explain our plans. While they go home to freeze the Popsicles, Uncle Reggie, Max, and I head directly to the community center, where Oliver and Elvis are trotting inside. "Dude!" Oliver calls across the parking lot. "Welcome back!" *It has been so long,* I think, *that he has forgotten Max's name.* But inside, people embrace us. Noodles's human pats the scruff of my neck while Elvis playfully nips at my muzzle. Even the sheepdog doesn't wreck the occasion; it squints at me but does not approach, its paws staying firmly on its side of the room.

"You've got this," Max tells me as we take our positions, as I waver before my showstopping jump. "Don't even think about it. Just go."

His arm quivers. My legs quiver. But I get a running start and jump for our friendship, jump for how hard we've worked, jump for everything that's riding on our performance now: the movie prize, our togetherness, our lives as we know it.

I nail the move. *We* nail the move.

Finally.

* ★

That night, we practice our dance in the cul-de-sac,

watch a program about rain forest frogs, and then Max cleans his teeth, petting my head with one hand, gripping the brush with the other. When he's in bed, Mom knocks on the door.

"You up?" she asks.

"You don't need to keep coming in here for lights-out," Max says, rolling his back toward her. "I'm not a baby anymore."

She pauses in the doorway. "Can we talk at least?"

Max shrugs, his shoulders ruffling the sheets.

"I'm just going to take that as a yes." She crosses her legs and sits next to me on the floor, stroking my ears. "I hope you had a nice conversation with your uncle. He loves you and he's worried about you. But I wanted to let you know that you can still talk to me, too—whenever you need to or want to, whenever you feel like it's time."

"I just . . ." Max says quietly. "I just didn't think it would happen like that. It was really slow and really quick at the same time. And part of me . . . part of me believed that everyone's parents fought."

"They do. Some just fight more than others. Daddy and I—he grew one way and I grew another."

Max spins around to face us. His eyes are puffy. "Why'd Dad have to leave, though? Why couldn't he

have, like, stayed on the couch or something?"

"Because we couldn't fix it."

"But he didn't . . . He didn't have to *leave*. And now everything's all messed up, and we don't really know where we're going to live, or if . . . or if Cosmo and I will . . ."

Mom's brow furrows, worry ticking across her face. "If Cosmo and you what?"

Will be together. Will be apart. Will be happy in the end.

Some dogs, to avoid danger or distress, fold themselves very small. I see this in Max, as he dips his chin to his chest and begins to sob. I have never seen him cry so hard—*feel* so hard.

"Oh, sweetheart," Mom says, hugging us both. Her eyes are streaming, too, and she rubs the streaks with her wrists. "I wish I could've spared you and Emmaline from all of this. I wish I could've planned my whole life, *our* whole lives, and had everything work out perfectly. I know it's a little scary now—because it's new and unfamiliar. But I can promise you that one thing will never, ever, *ever* change: I will always love you a million stars in the sky."

"I—I love you a million moon rocks," Max chokes out, and I think about Mom's words—about the unfa-

miliar, the unknown. I've always feared it: what I cannot see or fully understand. But sometimes the unknown is thrust upon us, and we have no choice but to dive in paws-first, believing that we will float in the end.

Mom stays for a while, reading us *Calvin and Hobbes*. When she finally flicks off the lights, she peers in my direction: a golden lump by the foot of the bed. "You know," she says, "sometimes I envy Cosmo's life. All he has to do is lie there and get fed."

Max closes his eyes, his words fading off into the near dark. "I think you'd be surprised."

We sleep well that night and awake to crows cawing in the bright sun. It's three days before the dance competition. Mom says that we can do anything— *anything*—we want.

So we launch a rocket.

In Sawyer Park, Max hunches over a jumble of wires and cords, which I am strictly instructed not to chew. His fingers are so fast and so agile. If I were a less self-assured dog, I might experience a twinge of jealousy—how he can build and build with thumbs, beautiful thumbs.

Max connects the last wire and clicks the metal door shut, backing up. "I don't know if this is going to

243

work," he says. "It's bigger than my science fair one."

"I'm proud of you anyway," Mom says, clutching Emmaline's hand. "That's what I tell everyone at work: my son's going to be an astronaut."

We count down together. *Ten, nine, eight . . .*

"Blast off!" Max shouts. The four of us watch the rocket take flight, shooting way, way into the air—until there is nothing above us but clouds and sky.

Over time, dancers develop a signature style. Some
are smooth: they glide effortlessly across the floor.
Some pop their legs very fast at odd angles. I wonder
how my dancing will evolve, how I will be remembered. Someday I hope to develop my own signature
move. *Show me "the Cosmo,"* a human will say!

And the dancer will do it.

We celebrate the rocket launch with pizza, as all
launches should be celebrated. I feel compelled to eat
several napkins alongside the crust. I cannot help it.
The day is just too full of possibility.

That night, on our last walk of the evening, Max
and I pause in the cul-de-sac, letting the summer wind

breeze right past us. By the way his fingers are twitching, I can tell he's practicing the hand cues for our big performance. He smells nervous. A thin sheen of sweat appears on his skin.

"Cosmo?" he asks suddenly, as I'm about to relieve myself by the mailbox. "I know I'm supposed to be confident about our dance, and I am—pretty much. We've learned a lot, and we're way better than when we started, but . . . now that the competition's so close, it feels really *real,* doesn't it? On Sunday, we need to dance the best we've ever danced."

He stares down at me, curls haloing his head, and I tell him that I want to dance heroically. If every dog has his day, I'd like for Sunday to be mine. Thanks to the wonderfully warm weather, the pain in my paw has almost disappeared, and I'm more limber than I've been in years.

"The most important thing is nailing that showstopper," Max says, breathing out. "The rest of the routine is one thing, but we're counting on that jump, Cosmo."

And I know it. I know how much is riding on me.

On Friday night, we practice and practice and *practice,* while Mom and Uncle Reggie spend hours at the sewing machine, crafting Max's letterman sweater for the dance competition. He will look just like Danny in the final scene of *Grease,* except on his sweater is an "M" for Max. Like on Halloween, Mom holds the fabric to the light and asks my opinion: "Whaddya think, Cosmo?"

I am thinking so many things, it is hard to settle on just one.

The sweater, however, is beautiful.

I, too, will dress to impress on Sunday. There was a great debate about my costume and how elaborate it should be. While I do not condone costumes for dogs on Halloween, I think that dancing requires an extra level of pizzazz. Mom sews a faux-leather bandanna, so I may be a T-Bird like Danny and Max. The costume does not require a hat, for which I am thankful.

The sewing machine is still rumbling when Dad calls. I can hear him and Max speaking in the other room: about the launch, about the dance contest. I'm not sure if Dad is coming on Sunday. Apparently, he has moved into what humans call a "condo." I have never heard the term, but based on Max's description, I imagine linoleum floors, flickering lights, and a kitchen with little space to twirl.

"Well," Max says, "um, okay, I'll see you soon then. Okay. Yeah, thanks. Bye."

When Max hangs up, I follow him into the bathroom, where the toilet lid is closed, and the toilet paper is wedged annoyingly into a corner. In front of the mirror, he tries on his letterman sweater. It falls easily over his shoulders. To give the full effect, he greases back his hair with strong-smelling gel. He is transformed! He is *Danny*!

And my costume—oh, my costume! When Max ties the leather fabric around my neck, I feel myself come alive. Often, on the Fourth of July, I see dogs in American flag bandannas, and I mock them. It's not nice of me, but I do. *It's an entrapment!* I bark. *Your neck should be free!*

How wrong I was. There is magic in this bandanna.

"You look awesome," Max says.

My new look has given me so much energy that, later in the evening, I half climb into the bathtub with Emmaline. She fashions me a "soap bubble hat," which I attempt to eat, but it is bitter. I get tired of smacking my tongue. Instead, I mouth one of her miniature ducks, though it does not squeak as loudly as Mr. Oinkers.

Mom appears in the doorway. "I was thinking. Cosmo could use a bath, too."

I cannot deny that my scent has become . . . pungent,

even to me. Generally I put little thought into my grooming, but for a dancer, attention to detail is everything. So I relent the next day. After going over our routine one final time, Max bathes me in the backyard, rubbing extra soap into my fur and washing me with a hose.

"Hold still," he keeps saying.

I try. But the competition is tomorrow, my stress level incredibly high—so I shake and shake, fur all over the place. Every second is one step closer to the dance floor, to the movie role, to proving that Max and I can never be apart.

By the swings, Emmaline is in a blue ruffled bathing suit, giggling and jumping through the sprinkler, the August sun beaming down. I bark, partly because the sprinkler is chasing her, partly because it looks like fun. Muddy water is pooling around my paws as I break free and do my best impression of a gallop toward Emmaline.

"Cosmooooo," Emmaline says, arms out to hug me, and we frolic in circles through the grass, trying to catch the sprinkler droplets in our mouths. I'm surprised when Max doesn't drag me back to my bath—but joins us, the three of us laughing and smiling until the sun goes down, the mosquitoes arrive, and we dry off for dinner.

I count myself lucky to be here with them, during the last warm breezes of summer. I'm not sure what will happen tomorrow—if we'll win, if Mom and Dad will see us in that movie, if we'll stay together in the end. But right now, I think we are happy.

After dark, Max brings out glass jars for fireflies. Boo comes over to play, immediately springing into the air and nipping at the little bugs with his teeth. He catches several, and wheezes very loudly as they become trapped in the back of his throat. For Emmaline, I do not place a single firefly in my mouth. My misdeed, all those years ago, is forgiven.

Then: tires crackling up the driveway, headlights on the lawn. Dad! He steps out of the car, chin low, and hugs Max and Emmaline. They stiffen—then sink into him. "Who's ready for ice cream?" he asks.

And I just can't believe it. I just can't believe he's here. I flop on my back, exposing my belly, my legs kicking into the air.

Max says, "We can bring Cosmo, right?"

And Dad says, "We can do anything you want."

We end up going to the stand in Sawyer Park, despite my warnings about the sheepdog. (It often goes on evening walks. How can we be so careless?) But Max gets strawberry ice cream and Emmaline

chooses vanilla, and Dad says he's missed us; he's missed us all so much. While Emmaline chases the last of the fireflies, cone teetering in her hands, Dad and Max plop down on a wooden bench. I pant by their feet, alert and watchful.

"I shouldn't have left like that," Dad says to Max, when Emmaline can't hear. "I think you're old enough to know this: Parents make mistakes. And I made a mistake, driving off that day. I should have stayed close by."

"But you're still getting divorced?" Max asks.

Dad nods. "Still getting divorced. I want you to know something, though." He clears his throat, watching the chocolate ice cream melt in his bowl. "The first time I saw your mother, I stopped breathing—she was that beautiful. I remember thinking I was the luckiest man in the world, that she even noticed me. That she *married* me. And I got to be your dad, and Emmaline's. Those things . . . I can never repay her for those things. That kind of love doesn't just go away. It's different now. But it doesn't go away."

The way Max and Dad are looking at each other, with their eyes so brown and warm, reminds me of how they were. They used to laugh. On Saturday mornings, they would watch funny cartoons that featured stupid birds. They would cook piles of waffles, then shoot basketballs in the driveway. I enjoyed chasing those balls, which were always rolling into inconvenient places, and I became an explorer, dashing after them into uncharted territory.

"Are you coming tomorrow?" Max asks.

"I . . . I don't want to miss it," Dad says. "But I'm trying to respect your mother's space. And I'm not sure that she wants me there right now."

Max contemplates this. "If I ask her and she says that it's okay, will you come?"

"I will." Dad ruffles Max's hair. "I love you, kiddo. You have no idea how much I love you."

"I love you, too," Max says, feeding me the end of his cone.

If the sheepdog is out there, in the depths of the park, I think it knows not to show its face tonight. I think it knows that we are strong—and tomorrow, we will be ready.

In bed that night, I toss. I turn.

"Couldn't sleep, either?" Max asks me when the sun is up, rubbing his eyes. We slip into our costumes, and I watch him brush his hair in the mirror. I watch his beautiful hands smooth the folds of his sweater. At breakfast, he picks at his waffles; I shove kibble around with my nose, poking a hole in the middle to give the impression that I have eaten. But my stomach won't allow it. When I'm anxious, I find it difficult to keep down food, and I shed, too. Great clouds float from me now as Max attaches my leash, as we settle into the minivan with deep sighs. I yawn to calm myself, which does little good, so I replay our routine in my mind.

We've worked incredibly hard for this moment.

I hope it's enough.

"Motown?" Mom asks. I'm not sure she fully grasps the magnitude of what's about to happen, how Max and I will encounter the sheepdog and leap into the unknown. But she seems rattled, too—smoothing one side of her hair over and over again. "Motown will help. Put you in the right spirit."

She turns up the music. As we drive, the great singer Aretha Franklin reminds me that our dance deserves R-E-S-P-E-C-T. According to Max, that spells *respect,* not *raccoon,* as I had previously guessed.

Emmaline chews on her cheek, watching the highway stream outside. "Is Daddy coming?"

"He is," Mom says, clearing her throat. "We spoke on the phone last night, and he told me that he wouldn't miss it." She peers in the rearview mirror. "Oh my goodness, Cosmo. You were *born* to wear that bandanna."

Light breaks through the open windows, a breeze tucking under my ears; I hold my head high, trying not to think about separation, about what will happen if Max and I lose this competition. Yet it's difficult to

think about anything else — so I stick my head out the window, attempting to lose myself in the wonderful battering of air.

The drive takes much longer than I expected, and in the end, we pull into a large parking lot with gravel that's rough underneath my paws. We're in another town, far from home, and I have never wished so much for the community center, for familiar ground. Strangers flock all around us: people in hats, people in matching T-shirts, people with bags of popcorn and cans of soda. I have little experience with carnivals — only what I've seen in *Grease* — but the atmosphere is similar. Everything is bright, chaotic. Everything pops.

"Stick close to me, Cosmo," Max says, nervous.

"Where do you sign in?" Mom asks, and we follow Max, who leads us on instinct: through the gathering crowd, past dog after well-groomed dog. I should say hello to everyone, greet everyone, but I'm doing my best to focus.

"I didn't know it would be this *big*," Max says to me as we slink into the stadium. This past year, I've been so focused on our dance that I never imagined — not once — where the competition would actually take place. But Max is right: the bleachers are gigantic. The football field gleams endlessly in the mid-August sun.

At the registration table, Emmaline squeezes Max's hand as he gives our names. "Max-and-Cosmo-Walker," he says, like we are one. The woman behind the table throws us a huge smile and passes over a badge, which Max sticks to my dog tags. He keeps tugging at the neckline of his sweater, as if his collar is too tight.

"Okay, looks like you've already given us your music, and you're up fourth," the table-woman says, "so break a leg!" I guess this is a human expression, but I don't care for it. My legs are already buckling.

"Where's Uncle Reggie?" Max asks, biting his thumbnail.

"He should be here already," Mom says, standing on her toes and peering above the crowd. "Let me give him a call."

"Mommy," Emmaline says, "can I have some popcorn?"

And I can tell Max is incredibly anxious now, his eyes mostly on the grass, which is the stiff type—and very, very green.

Mom nods, adjusting the camera bag on her shoulder. "Of course, sweetheart. After we find your uncle."

"You can just get some popcorn now," Max says, "if you want."

"Don't be silly," Mom says. "We'll wait with you."

"No, really. I . . . Cosmo and I have to warm up and practice our routine at least once more before we perform. It's okay. I can see you after the show."

Mom furrows her eyebrows, uncertain. "Are you sure?"

Max says *yes,* he is—and I understand that he wants a few minutes, just the two of us. So Mom kisses the smooth crown of Max's head, telling him, "You'll do great," while Emmaline says, "*Cosmooooo,* good luck." As they trail toward the popcorn stand, weaving through the crowd, I try to memorize the way they walk together, stride for small stride.

Soon, the sound of barking outweighs everything else.

We run over the choreography briefly, focusing on ourselves, but around us are young dogs, flashy dogs, also warming up. They spring; they spin and bounce, leapfrogging over their humans, punching the sky.

"They're good," Max says, confirming my fears. "Maybe we should go over our routine one more time."

"*But first,*" Uncle Reggie says behind us, "you

need to see my costume." We turn around, and there he is—a T-Bird, too. He's smiling his bulldog smile. "Man, I've been looking for you guys everywhere."

"You dressed up for us?" Max asks in disbelief.

Uncle Reggie winks. "You think I wouldn't? Now, about this dance . . ."

We practice the whole thing again, nailing every aspect, while Uncle Reggie cheers us on. "Perfect," he says. "Perfection!"

Right before the competition begins, Oliver and Elvis stop by to wish us good luck. They're swathed in green, with feathers in their hats. *"Peter Pan,"* Oliver tells us. "You know the song 'You Can Fly!'?"

I do not. But if Elvis has achieved such a feat, I'm thrilled for him.

A voice rings out over the loudspeaker. "Ladies! Gentlemen! Dogs! All contestants please make their way to the center of the field." Whoops and yips follow, along with a sharp bark from Noodles. Even above the crowd, I can hear her—and *see* her, sprinting around in a tiny lion costume, her human at her heels.

That's when I spot it: a very large tuft of gray-and-white fur, tumbling toward my paws. The sheepdog? The fur ball fully approaches me, guided by the breeze,

and I take a whiff. The sheepdog! Just the smell of it throws my hackles up.

"Quickly, quickly!" the loudspeaker voice says.

Suddenly the demon is right beside me, ribbons on its collar. It looks composed. Confident. And it smiles as I release a full-throated growl.

"Come on," Max is saying, guiding me to center field, and Uncle Reggie is calling after us, "You've got this! You've *got* this!"

Blades of grass crunch beneath our paws. Max tugs at his sweater again, a bead of sweat on his nose. And I'm telling the demon with every step, every whip of my tail: *We are strong.*

"Welcome, everyone!" says the loudspeaker. "We are so happy that you could make it to the First Annual Rainy-Day Dance Society's Canine Freestyle Championship! Woo, that's a mouthful, isn't it? We've got twenty-six awesome dogs here today, and everyone's worked really hard, so can we show them all some love?"

The audience hoots and claps, but I refuse to take my eyes off the sheepdog.

"Please also welcome our judges," the loudspeaker says, "who have a *very* important job today, because the winning team gets, as you know, a *big* movie prize! Each dog will perform for roughly two minutes, and if you could hold all applause until the end of each routine, that would be wonderful. Now, everyone please move to the sidelines except for our first contestants—Melinda Rogers and her sheepdog, Comet!"

The sheepdog? *Comet?*

I was not prepared for it to have a name. What's more, the demon's name is of the universe—just like mine. The odds are so astounding that I cannot begin to comprehend them. I shiver, ears flattening. After we skulk to the sidelines, Uncle Reggie asks Max, "Hey, doesn't that dog live in your neighborhood?"

Live in the neighborhood? It terrorizes the neighborhood! It's a plague on our houses!

The sheepdog's music begins, softly at first, and I recognize the tune immediately: "Singin' in the Rain," from one of my favorite dance films. It irks me, to see a classic defiled like this. The sheepdog prances menacingly, flicking its paws with abandon. As the chorus swells, it wobbles on its hind legs, standing monstrously tall. And yet—I'll admit that there is something graceful about it. Something pure. For a few moments, I get swept up in its beauty, in the flow and swish of its fur. A terrible spell? The sheepdog must have cast a spell over the audience, over me.

The song booms. Two of the judges are tapping their fingers to the beat, and I realize in horror that one of them is wearing a fluffy sweater, like Grandma and Grandpa do. This judge must be on the side of the sheepdog; swaying them will be difficult.

When the song ends, a hush of admiration swells throughout the crowd. Max claps, but I can tell he's grown even more nervous; his eyes are watering. How do we beat a dog that walks like a human?

"You have more heart than that," Uncle Reggie tells us on the sidelines, as if he's reading our thoughts. "Don't focus on anyone else but you, though. The best that you can do is more than enough."

Max bites his lip and peers into the stands. "You haven't seen my dad yet, have you?"

Uncle Reggie looks around. "He's probably just running a little late, bud."

I notice that this is not really an answer.

A border collie performs next, then a German shepherd—but neither of their routines are as strong as the sheepdog's. There's a trickle of applause from the audience, and we wait. Waiting is the worst part.

"Next up," the loudspeaker finally says, "we have Max Walker and his golden retriever, Cosmo!"

"Go, Max and Cosmo!" Mom shouts from the stands, hands cupped around her mouth.

And Emmaline yells, "You can do it!"

If Max were a dog, I believe he would be shedding profusely. Right after the announcement, I start to smell sweat on his palms. He bends down to adjust my bandanna. "Can I tell you something?"

Always, I say, bridging the space between us, shoving my muzzle into his face.

"I think I like hanging out with you more than anyone else."

And I, you.

"You know I really want us to win, because I never want to be separated from you—ever. But . . . I also want you to know, even if we don't win, I'm still happy I'm here with you. You're my best friend, and I hope that everyone sees that." He kisses the top of my head, and I sit up very, very tall.

Uncle Reggie asks us, "Ready?"

And we are. We are.

We make our way to the center of the field, our hearts thumping to the claps of the crowd. Ears cocked, I stand frozen—just waiting for it—and watch Max's mouth form words.

"I'm nervous," he whispers.

Me, too, I think.

But when the song starts, I just *feel.* Feel my paws marching and shuffling. Feel the spring of the grass, the thickness of the air. I begin my series of elaborate twirls as Max circles me in the opposite direction. The world narrows to us and the music.

Max snaps his fingers and shuffles toward the audience, mimicking the movie scene with wonderful precision, and I hope that judges will see — I hope the judges are *seeing* — that together we are perfect for the big screen. As the chorus kicks in, Max actually starts singing the lyrics, which he's never done in practice; I wish I understood the words enough to sing along with him. Even with this addition, his moves are fluid where they need to be. Crisp where they should be. We dip and spin and prance in unison, so the judges will understand that we are one.

On the sidelines, Uncle Reggie is looking incredibly focused, nodding his head as I walk backward, roll over, shake my hindquarters.

"Woo!" Oliver shouts, and Elvis barks his approval.

Max is smiling. Actually smiling.

As we near the middle of our dance, I'm throwing everything I have into it; I'm calling upon all my skills, digging as deep as I can, focusing on Max's blurred hands. And it occurs to me that I do not have to be fearless. Sometimes worry stays beneath your fur, in the small spaces that fear likes to hide—but I do believe that, with the right human by your side, it's possible to leap fearlessly into the unknown.

That's what we are doing, Max and I.

We are taking a leap.

And this bond between us will never change. Some day in the future, the two of us might be apart—maybe not for long, maybe only by a couple of miles—but when I see him in the distance, I will hobble over, and he will cradle my head in his hands, those hands that have built things, and grown things, and danced so beautifully.

Maybe I'm slower than the other dogs, wobblier than the other dogs—maybe my hips aren't moving exactly the way we practiced. But Max! Max is a star, and I think he knows he's shining, like he did on dance nights. His hands move like Danny's in the jive scene. His feet are lighter than duck feathers. The first time I saw him, I knew he was brilliant. I knew I would protect him, doggedly. Love him, fiercely.

I will. I do.

We dance.

Some people in the audience begin clapping to the beat. I steal a glance at Mom, whose hands are pressed together at her lips.

As we near the big move, my left paw is aching; my muscles are so sore. But I take a running start anyway, and stretch my legs out anyway, and leap anyway. Max stoops down, reaching his arm to the side—and I don't clear it. In fact, I'm nowhere near. My paws skim the ground. I crash into his shoulder, knocking him back. The audience gasps; some of the judges wince. We both tumble slightly to the ground, but it's the end of the song now, and we must bow. It takes everything I have not to collapse by Max's feet.

But I've done my best, my very best.

"Yeah!" Uncle Reggie is shouting, rushing onto the field to embrace us. "Get it, *yeah!*"

For a moment I'm afraid that our dance has reached him and only him. Then it happens. People are standing. *Everyone* is standing, clapping and clapping for us. I know it isn't because I danced with skill, but because we danced with heart.

Max, Uncle Reggie, and I—we laugh. We laugh and hug each other, although nothing is funny, and I'm almost scared to look into the stands. But I look

anyway, and there they are, the three of them. Mom, Dad, and Emmaline, standing together. *Dancing together.* Dad holds Mom's hand and spins her. She tucks neatly under his arm, her curls bouncing.

And I remember one of the last lines of *Grease*.

How could I have forgotten?

"Oh, look! Oh, the gang's together."

Three weeks later, silver trailers glint all around us.
Max and I are back, on the same field as the dance
competition, but it's been transformed: we see folding
chairs and cameras, megaphones and boxes of lights.
A real live movie set.

Max can't stop grinning—even though we did not
win the grand prize for our performance. According to
the judges, our showstopping mishap cost us a bundle
of points, and we placed very near the bottom. But
afterward, there were hands on our shoulders, and
words from a man in a striking black hat: *Charisma!*
You have such charisma! Would you like to be in the
film, too?

It must be said that the sheepdog won and spent the next four days prancing around the neighborhood with a massive blue ribbon on its collar. Although I'm no champion—there is no ribbon assigned to my name—I'm still proud of what Max and I accomplished. I'm proud that it got us here.

"I think someone wants to say hello," Max says as we're settling into our spot on the sidelines. And it's the sheepdog, taking step after tentative step in our direction. *We should face each other,* I think, *once and for all.*

Max following a safe distance behind me, I strut over, fully expecting the monster dog to come charging. I bark mightily.

The sheepdog barks back.

Then it does something wholly unexpected: it bows. Is this a trick? It must be a trick! Why else would the sheepdog bow in friendship, if not to throw me off? Yet it bows again, playfully hopping forward, its tongue drifting out the side of its mouth. What about the glowing eyes? What about the evil in its soul?

I approach the sheepdog with extreme caution, my paws dragging across the grass. Its jaw is relaxed. Beneath its wisps of fur, there are eyes as smooth and calm as a goose-less pond.

The sheepdog's human steps forward, wearing a loose shirt and stretchy pants, her hair frizzing around her ears. "About time you two met," she says, dropping to one knee in front of me. Her hands smell like Mom's flower sprays. "I knew I was going to like you."

She turns to the sheepdog, nuzzling its head.

So I take a chance—edging closer and closer to the sheepdog, until we are nose to nose. I lick Comet's face. She licks mine. And it erases everything between us. Suddenly we're playing like puppies, rolling in the grass, wild and untamed.

"Good dogs," Comet's human says, laughing.

"Cosmo," Max adds, "looks like you've made a friend."

And I have. No matter how old I become, I'm still learning. The world is still opening my eyes. If it were up to me, I'd live a hundred more years—or even twenty, or ten. I would like to watch Max continue to grow, watch him graduate from school and live in a house of his own; and hopefully, if I was lucky, we'd get together and reminisce. About turkey bacon at breakfast. About couch cushions that sunk too low. About dancing in our cul-de-sac during a mild summer rain. But I will settle for this. I will settle for these moments, when the mysterious becomes familiar,

when everything and anything feels possible.

Mom and Uncle Reggie appear right before the director says, "Cast members, get in place!" As Max and I approach the middle of the set, ready to dance with Comet, Mom calls after us. Her voice rings through the early September air.

"Remember! You belong together!"

She's talking about the song.

She's also talking about us.

And we have done it. I think that Max and I have done it.

The cameras roll. First, everything is quiet and perfect and still—then the change comes: the movement and the flow. Max jives; Max leaps; Max shines.

This much I know: he will have this forever. *We* will have this forever. A cool blue sky, a football field in the beginning of autumn, the two of us performing a one-two step across the green, green grass. One day, when Max is old and gray like me, these memories will strike him. He might be flying in a rocket ship, or shopping for cereal, or playing softly in a pile of leaves—and he will stop, our movie scene unfolding itself before him.

In a whisper, he will say my name.

Evening breaks. Flashlights race across the ground. It seems like so long since last Halloween, but here we are again. My ears perk at the sounds of trick-or-treaters rushing through the cul-de-sac. Somewhere in the night, my friend Comet howls; it is no longer a frightful noise.

"Look at *you,* Cosmo," Max says to me, crouching down on his knees to rub my head. Instead of a turtle, I am a T-Bird again, and Max is an astronaut. He wears a puffy white suit and carries a helmet in the crook of his arm. We are exactly who we should be.

From the mailbox, Emmaline waves at us in her Sandy costume: miniature leather jacket, hair poofy like a poodle. "We're gonna miss all the good candy!" she says, shifting from one foot to another.

"I promise," Uncle Reggie says. "This neighborhood has *plenty* of good candy." He whistles for his dog, Rosie, who charges from behind the squirrel bushes, the turtle shell strapped to her back. She doesn't despise the costume as much as I did—she's even wearing the hat. We play gently for a moment, the two of us bowing in the chill of the yard.

"Hold on a minute," Max says to Emmaline. "We're waiting for Dad."

Mom finishes lighting the strange pumpkin on the porch. "I'm not exactly sure if your dad's —"

But her words stop as she sees headlights pulling into the driveway. Dad steps out of his car. He is dressed, from what I can tell, as himself. "Sorry I'm late," he says to everyone. "Traffic was brutal."

I rush up to him—as fast as I can, which is not too fast at all. Every time Dad sees me, my muzzle is a bit whiter. But I am strong. I feel so strong.

"Hey, boy," he says. "I've missed you! It's been a long couple of days."

We spend half the week with Dad, and half the week with Mom: a shared custody. All of us, together. The day after we filmed our movie scene, Mom promised she'd

never split us up. "I double-pinkie swear," she said, which pleased me. Humans value their pinkies; I took her at her word.

Emmaline hugs Dad and then hurries us along. "Now can we go? Please! I don't want raisins again!"

Max says, "I *would* like some M&M's."

So we march into the night, cool air against our fur, and I marvel at how much love there is between us. Love, still. It took me fourteen years to figure it out, but here is what I know, more than anything else. We will always be a family. Families grow and evolve—but I will never stop being Max's brother. Dad will never stop being Max's father. We are connected in all ways, big and small. I take great comfort in that.

Perhaps Max senses that I'm slowing down, because he turns back to look at me. There is so much brightness on his face. "You can do it, boy."

I follow Max. I pick up the pace.

After him—*for* him—I feel like I could run forever.

ACKNOWLEDGMENTS

I, Cosmo is the absolute book of my heart. Dogs have always been my best friends, and I'm very thankful for the opportunity to write about just how special they are. I don't know where I'd be—or who I'd be—without my childhood dog, Sally. I don't know how I would have survived middle school without my golden retriever, Ralphie. And I am grateful for each and every moment with my American dingo, Dany, no matter how many times a day she drags me to the dog park. (Hint: many, many times.)

If you're reading this, you probably love dogs just as much as I do. That makes you a special human, indeed. Thank you for being wonderful.

To my literary agent, Claire Wilson, for believing in Cosmo (and in me) from his very first dance steps; you are a star! To Tom Bonnick, for shaping this book with wisdom, brilliance, and care—and for letting me blab about my dog, over and over again, during our editorial calls. To Susan Van Metre, for her insight, superb editorial guidance, and obvious love for Cosmo; thank you for betting on us. All three of you have made this journey a deliriously happy one. Everyone at RCW, Nosy Crow, and Walker Books also deserves a big round of app-paws. (Sorry, that was a terrible pun. But you really are lovely people.)

Sandy Johnson, thank you for being my neighbor; your support for this book has meant so much to me. Erin Cotter, bless you for your uplifting WhatsApp messages and emotional support during Dany's puppy stage! And Ellen, for asking about Cosmo and for guerrilla marketing in Barnes & Noble. I am lucky to know such strong women. In that same vein, to everyone who's encouraged me during this project, including Grandma Pat, Miss Kim, the staff at McIntyre's, and my dog park friends: you have kept me afloat more than you know.

My eternal thanks to the Atlanta Humane Society, who helped bring Dany into my life.

Cosmo came from a breeder, but if you're looking to adopt a dog, I would encourage everyone to first look at shelters and rescues. There are so many good dogs who need homes; your best friend is waiting to meet you!

Thank you, Jago, for reading *I, Cosmo*'s early pages on a train, and for texting me to say, *This is the best thing you've ever written.* To Dad, for your Ralphie voice (*Hullo!*), and for chuckling—in your knowing way—when I told you about this book. And to Mom, always Mom, for filling our house with animals, for talking with me endlessly about Cosmo, and for teaching me what it means to love, doggedly, with all your heart.

Carlie Sorosiak grew up in North Carolina. She has a master's in English from Oxford University and another in creative writing and publishing from City, University of London. She is the author of two novels for young adults, *If Birds Fly Back* and *Wild Blue Wonder*. Her life goals include traveling to all seven continents and fostering a wide variety of animals. She lives in Atlanta with her husband, Jago, and their American dingo, Dany.